ISBN: 979-8-9928349-1-8

The Night I Choose Myself

DEDICATION

This is for you.

Yes, **you.**

Especially you. You know who you are. Don't act surprised—yes, I'm talking to you.

You, the one who inspired this, the one who made me laugh, cry, and question every decision I've ever made. The one who reminded me that life is both heartbreakingly beautiful and hilariously unpredictable.

This book? It's yours.

For every late-night overthinker, for the lovers of love, the fearless and the fearful, the ones who have danced in joy and stumbled through sorrow. For the ones who keep choosing themselves, even on the days it feels impossible.

May you always know that your story is yours to write—and that sometimes, the best chapters start with a little bit of chaos.

To the ones who have ever felt lost, uncertain, or unworthy—

This book is for you.

For the ones who have given too much, loved too deeply, and lost themselves in the process. For the ones who have struggled to see their own worth, who have chased validation in places that could never hold them, who have learned love the hard way.

For those who have walked away from what no longer served them, even when it hurt. For those who are still learning to choose themselves, still learning to stand in their own light, still learning that they are enough—exactly as they are.

This book is a love letter to you.

To your strength, your resilience, your courage to begin again.

May you always remember that your story is yours to write.

EPIGRAPH

"There comes a night when you stop searching for love in others and start choosing yourself. Not because you stopped believing in love, but because you finally realized that the love you've been waiting for has always been within you."

— Kessa Alcenat

Foreword

There are books that entertain, books that inform, and then there are books that find you when you need them most—whispering truths you've been too afraid to say out loud.

This is one of those books.

I did not write this to tell a love story; I wrote this to tell the truth—the kind of truth that aches before it sets you free. The truth of losing yourself in someone else. The truth of longing for love so desperately that you forget you are already worthy of it. And the truth of what happens when you finally stop searching for home in others and start building it within yourself.

If you have ever loved and lost, if you have ever questioned your worth, if you have ever stood at the crossroads between who you were and who you are becoming—this book is for you.

And if you have ever needed permission to choose yourself, let this be it.

Welcome to *The Night I Chose Myself.*

— Kessa Alcenat

Preface

Finding Myself Again

There was a time when I believed love was the answer to everything. That love—when given or received—could mend every wound, fill every void, quiet every fear. I thought that love was the thing that defined us, that made life whole, that turned loneliness into belonging. I shaped myself around this idea, molding my heart to fit the expectations of others, believing that if I gave enough, if I stayed enough, if I loved enough, then I would be enough.

But love, as I once knew it, did not save me. Instead, it broke me open. It forced me to see the cracks I had ignored, the fractures in my own identity that no relationship could mend. It made me realize that I had spent so much time searching for love outside of myself that I had forgotten how to find it within me.

This is not a story about finding someone else. This is a story about finding myself again.

The Journey of Becoming

I did not wake up one morning and decided to let go of everything I once believed. Growth does not happen in grand, sweeping gestures. It happens in the quiet moments—the pauses between heartbreak and healing, the space between endings and new beginnings. It happens when you sit with yourself long enough to hear the questions you've been avoiding, when you stop running and start listening to the voice you have silenced for too long.

For me, that voice whispered truths I had been too afraid to face. That love is not something to chase. That being alone does not mean being unloved. That happiness is not something another person hands to you—it is something you build, something you nurture, something you choose.

And so, I chose myself. Not because I no longer believed in love, but because I finally understood that love begins here, within me. That must be rooted in self-acceptance, in self-trust, in the quiet confidence of knowing that I am enough—without validation, without permission, without anyone else's presence to make it real.

A Story Worth Writing

This book is not just about love and loss, about heartbreak and healing. It is about transformation. It is about the man who learned how to stand on his own, who walked away not because he stopped loving, but because he started loving himself more. It is about the courage it takes to choose yourself, even when the world tells you that love should come first.

It is also about the mistakes we make when we do not yet know how to love ourselves. About how fear, insecurity, and the weight of our past can drive us to hurt the very things we hold most dear. I once believed that love could only survive if I proved myself worthy of it, if I controlled it, if I could be what I thought another person needed me to be. And in that desperate need to be enough, I made choices that shattered the very love I had tried to protect.

I let my insecurities whisper lies, let them convince me that I was unworthy of the kind of love that stayed. I let fear make my choices for me, pushing away the one person who had seen me completely and loved me anyway. And when I lost him, I thought I had lost everything.

But in losing her, I found myself.

This is a story about the consequences of self-doubt, about the way we sabotage love when we do not believe we deserve it. But more importantly, it is about the redemption that follows—the moment you stop punishing yourself for the past and start learning how to forgive, how to heal, how to rebuild.

It is about rewriting the narrative, one where love is not the destination, but a companion on the journey. One where self-worth is not measured by who stays, but by who you become when you stand alone. One where endings are not failures, but invitations to begin again.

This is my story. And for the first time, I am the one writing it.

The Night I Choose Myself

Introduction

There comes a moment in life—not loud, not earth-shattering, but quiet. A moment when the weight of every choice, every love, every loss settles into the spaces you tried to ignore. And in that stillness, you realize you have spent so much time searching for home in others; you forgot to build one within yourself.

This is not just a story of love. It is a story of the nights that broke me, the mornings that remade me, and the days in between when I stood at the crossroads of who I was and who I was meant to become. It is about learning that love—real, unwavering love—does not ask you to shrink, to wait, to beg. It does not live in the hands of those who could never hold you fully. It is found in the reflection of the person who has been with you all along.

So, I chose myself. Not because love is unworthy, but because I am.

This is my story. Maybe it's yours, too

Prologue

There comes a night when silence is louder than any voice, when the echoes of every choice you've made press against your chest like an ocean that refuses to let you breathe.

You sit with the weight of it all—the love you lost, the mistakes you swore you'd never make, the truth you buried beneath excuses and time. And at that moment, there is no one left to blame, no distractions to soften the ache. Just you and the undeniable fact that somewhere along the way, you forgot yourself in the pursuit of being enough for someone else.

This is the story of that night.

The night I stood at the edge of who I was and who I could become. That night I realized that love, no matter how deep, cannot be borrowed, begged for, or proven. It must be found in the spaces you once abandoned within yourself.

And so, I did the only thing left to do.

I chose me.

Contents

The Night I Choose Myself

ACKNOWLEDGMENTS

I would like to express my deepest gratitude to the many individuals who have supported me throughout the writing of "The Night, I Chose Myself."

First and foremost, to my mother, Yolette Alcenat, whose unwavering encouragement and the powerful reminder to "look at yourself in the mirror" fueled my determination. Her belief in me was a constant source of inspiration... To my sister, Elvire P. Stanislous, a beacon of strength, courage, and determination. You've been like a second mother to me, demonstrating the power of resilience and unwavering spirit. Your example has been a constant source of motivation...And to my brother, Ernst Alcenat, for his unwavering support and belief in my creative endeavors.

To my dear friends Millerson Paul and Jimmy Louis, thank you for your inspiring words and for reminding me that my "nice pen" has the power to touch others.

"To my amazing team, Pavlo, Altanas, Eliude, Leica, Ryan, Nazaneo, and Kaysen, thank you for your unwavering support and dedication. Despite your best efforts to distract me with video games and requests for endless snacks, you somehow allowed me to finish this book. Thanks for the "inspiration"… Your collaborative spirit and hard work made this book possible."

Finally, to all my readers, thank you for your support. Your interest and engagement mean the world to me. I hope you find something within these pages that resonates with you.

The Night I Choose Myself

1 The beginning of the end

Alina's Perspective

I told myself I had forgotten her. That the years had buried every memory, every whispered promise, every piece of her that once lived inside me. But then I saw her again. And the past hit me like a blade, sharp and unforgiving.

Lucian Monroe.

She stood at the far end of the café, her dark brown hair falling in soft waves over her shoulders, fingers wrapped around a cup of coffee like it was the only thing keeping her steady. The café was alive with the murmur of voices, the hiss of steamed milk swirling into espresso, the clinking of ceramic cups against saucers. Yet, in that moment, the world faded, sound dulled, time seemed to narrow until it was just the two of us again, standing on opposite ends of something broken.

For a second, she was just another person in the crowd. Then she turned, and our eyes met. And just like that, the past became the present.

"Lucian."

Her voice didn't shake. It wasn't fragile or uncertain. It was exactly as I remembered—smooth, warm, like it belonged to someone who still believed in the power of love. I resented that I recognized it instantly. It still made something shift inside me.

I said nothing at first, just watched her, waiting for the regret to flicker in her eyes. It did. That pleased me. I wanted her to feel it. Because I had. Every single day since she left. She had no right to look at me like that. No right to bring this weight crashing back down on my shoulders after all this time. But the past had never played fair. And neither had she.

Lucian's Perspective

The cafe was bustling, a symphony of clinking cups and murmuring conversations. I sat in my usual corner, lost in the pages of a book, trying to ignore the dull ache in my chest that had become my constant companion.

Then, I saw her.

Alina.

Across the room, her back to me, but I would recognize that silhouette anywhere. The way her shoulders sloped, the curve of her neck, the way her hair fell in waves down her back. Time seemed to stop, the noise fading away as I watched her. My heart hammered against my ribs, a frantic drumbeat against the cage of my carefully constructed indifference. I hadn't seen her in years, yet here she was, as if she had never left.

She pivoted, and our eyes met. The years melted away, and for a fleeting moment, it was as if nothing had changed. The same warmth, the same vulnerability, the same spark that had drawn me to her all those years ago. But the warmth was quickly replaced by a surge of bitterness. The past, buried beneath layers of resentment and regret, clawed its way to the surface.

She had no right to be here, no right to disrupt the fragile peace I had built for myself.

"Lucian," she said, her voice a soft echo of a past I had tried to forget.

I wanted to ignore her; to pretend I hadn't seen her, to turn the page and disappear back into the world of my book. But I couldn't. The past had a way of demanding to be acknowledged, and Alina, even after all this time, still held a power over me that I couldn't deny.

Alina's Perspective

She hesitated. A flicker of uncertainty betrayed the carefully constructed composure she always wore. Alina Monroe had always been good at wearing masks, but this one cracked just enough for me to see through it.

"Lucian," she said again, softer this time, as if that would make a difference.

I forced myself to breathe, to steady the burn in my chest. My hands curled into fists beneath the table. "Alina."

It wasn't a greeting. It was a statement. A confirmation of her existence in front of me. A name that still holds too much history, too much weight.

She took a step closer, slow, tentative, like she wasn't sure if I'd let her. My pulse pounded, my mind already screaming at me to leave, to escape before she unraveled the stitches I had so carefully sewn over the years. But I didn't move. I should have.

Instead, I let my eyes drift over her—slowly, deliberately, memorizing details I shouldn't have cared about. The faint smudge of eyeliner beneath her lashes. The way her coat hung loosely off her shoulders like she had been in too much of a hurry to wear it properly. The small tremor in her fingers that she was trying so hard to hide.

She was nervous. She should be.

Lucian's Perspective

She moved closer, her hesitation betraying the carefully constructed composure she always wore. I watched her, my gaze tracing the familiar lines of her face, the way her eyes crinkled when she smiled, the way her lips curved when she spoke. The years had changed her, but not enough. The essence of Alina, the woman who had captured my heart and then shattered it, was still there. And the sight of her, so close, so vulnerable, reawakened a longing I had tried to bury.

It angered me that she could still make my heart ache, even after all this time. I resented that she could still make me question everything. But beneath the hate, a hint of hope stirred, perhaps. Or maybe just the desperate yearning for a past that could never be reclaimed.

Alina's Perspective

She reached for her coffee, took a sip, and then set it back down with a quiet clink. "Lucian," she started again, but I cut her off.

"No," I said, shaking my head. "You don't get to walk in here and act like we're just two old friends catching up. You made your choice, Alina."

She flinched, just barely. "I know," she repeated, her voice softer now. "But I also know that walking away from you was the hardest thing I've ever done."

I let out a humorless laugh. "You didn't walk away. You ran."

Her lips parted like she wanted to argue, but she didn't. Because she knew I was right.

The silence between us stretched, thick and suffocating, but I refused to be the one to break it. Let her sit with the weight of her own words. A flash of memory hit me—one I hadn't allowed myself to revisit in years. A summer night. The scent of jasmine in the air. Alina laughing as she danced barefoot on the sand, her fingers laced with mine, the ocean whispering at our feet. That was before everything fell apart. Before trust shattered like glass under the weight of doubt and deception. Before I realized she had never truly been mine. I pushed the memory away. That version of her was gone. And I refused to be haunted by her ghost.

Lucian's Perspective

Her words, laced with regret, were a punch to the gut. I watched her, my heart a battlefield of conflicting emotions. Anger. Hurt. Longing. She was right. Walking away—or rather, running away—had been the hardest thing she had ever done. But it had also been the most necessary. The silence between us was deafening, filled with the ghosts of unspoken words and unfulfilled promises. I wanted to lash out, to hurt her the way she had hurt me. But a part of me, the part that still loved her, held me back. Memories flooded my mind, unbidden and unwelcome. The laughter, the whispered secrets, the stolen kisses. The way she used to look at me, like I was the only man in the world. I closed my eyes, trying to shut out the images, the emotions. But the past had a way of clinging to you, refusing to let go.

Alina's Perspective

I should have left then. Instead, I stayed, trapped in the moment, in the memories unraveling around me. My mind spiraled back to the beginning—when we were new, untouched by doubt. When Alina looked at me like I was the only thing that mattered. And then, just as quickly as I remembered the end. The nights I spent questioning where she was. The way her words became rehearsed, lacking the warmth they once carried. The growing distance between us, the one I tried so hard to ignore.

“Why now?” I asked, finally breaking the silence.

She inhaled sharply, as she hadn't expected the question. "Because I couldn't keep pretending you don't exist. Because—” She stopped herself. As if the truth was too heavy to say aloud. But I already knew. And I wasn't about to make it easy for her.

“You think that matters now?” I scoffed, shaking my head. “You think after everything, after the way you left, you can just walk back into my life and expect me to listen?”

Her jaw tightened. "I never expected you to listen. But that doesn't mean I don't regret it."

Regret. I rolled the word around in my mind, tasting the bitterness of it. She regretted it. That was something, wasn't it? But then why had she done it?

Lucian's Perspective

Her question, "Why now?", hung in the air, heavy with unspoken meaning. I knew why she was here. The guilt had become too much.

2 If regret had a face

I should have expected this moment. For years, I played out a thousand versions of it in my mind. What would I say if I ever saw him again? How would I look at him? How would he look at me? But none of them felt like this. None of them prepared me for the way Lucian Laurent was looking at me now—like I was nothing but a memory he had already erased. And maybe I was. But that didn't make it hurt any less.

"Lucian."

I said his name as an apology. Like maybe if I said it softly enough, he wouldn't hear the regret woven into it. He didn't answer right away. Just stared at me, something cold and unreadable settling behind his gray eyes. And for the first time since I walked away from him all those years ago, I realized—I had lost him.

I gripped the coffee cup tighter, willing the warmth to steady my trembling hands. I had thought about this moment, imagined it countless times, but nothing had prepared me for the way my chest ached under the weight of his silence. He was different. Not just in the way he carried himself, but in the way he looked at me—like he had built walls so high that I would never be able to reach him again. And maybe that was the worst part. Knowing I had done this. Knowing that I had been the one to turn him into this man—so distant, so untouchable.

The air between us thickened, stretching out with years of unsaid words. I wanted to fill it, to mend it, but the damage had already been done. I did it. I closed my eyes for a brief second, gathering the courage to say what I had never been able to before. "I made a mistake, Lucian. A terrible one. And I've lived with it every day since."

His gaze didn't waver, didn't soften. "And what do you expect me to do with that?"

I swallowed hard. "Nothing. I don't expect anything. I just needed you to know."

A bitter chuckle escaped his lips. "I knew, Alina. I knew the moment you left. The only difference is, now you do too."

I longed to reach for him, to bridge the impossible distance between us. But I knew better.

Lucian's fingers tapped against the table, slow, deliberate. "Did you ever love him?"

The question stole the air from my lungs. My thoughts scrambled, searching for an answer that wouldn't hurt more than it already had.

"I tried to," I whispered.

He exhaled sharply, shaking his head. "That's not the same thing."

No, it wasn't. And we both knew it.

"I thought…" My voice wavered. "I thought if I walked away from you first, it wouldn't hurt as much when you eventually left me."

Lucian's expression didn't change, but something behind his eyes shifted. "And did it?"

The truth lodged itself in my throat, thick and unrelenting. I blinked rapidly, trying to push back the sting of tears. "No."

"Then you were a coward, Alina. You didn't protect yourself. You just hurt us both."

His words were sharp, but there was no anger in them. Just the truth. A truth I had known for years but never dared to admit. Silence wrapped around us, heavy and suffocating. Lucian looked past me, out the window, his jaw clenching as if he were fighting something unseen. "I don't know what you want from me, Alina."

"I don't know either," I admitted. "Maybe just… one last moment. One last truth."

He let out a tired sigh, rubbing his temples before meeting my gaze again. "You don't need my forgiveness."

"But do I have it?" I asked, my voice barely whispered.

Lucian stared at me for a long time before answering, his voice quiet, almost resigned. "Maybe some things aren't meant to be forgiven."

I should have left then. I should have let the finality of his words sink in and walked away. But I didn't. Instead, I lingered, my fingers tightening around my coffee cup as if it could somehow anchor me to this moment. I had spent years rehearsing all the things I would say if I ever got the chance to stand in front of him again, but none of them seemed right now. None of them seemed enough.

"I never stopped thinking about you," I admitted.

Lucian's gaze didn't flicker. "That doesn't change anything."

"I know," I whispered. "But it's the truth."

He let out a slow breath, rubbing a hand across his jaw. For the first time since I sat down, I saw something flicker in his expression—something raw, something unguarded. But it was gone just as quickly as it had appeared, replaced by the same unreadable mask he had worn when I first walked in.

"You made your choice, Alina. And now you have to live with it."

His words were final. And yet, I couldn't let them be the last ones between us.

"Do you hate me?" I asked, my voice barely whispered.

Lucian's jaw tightened. "I don't think about you enough to hate you."

A sharp pain bloomed in my chest at his words, but I forced myself to nod. "That's fair."

Silence settled between us again, heavier this time. The café around us bustled with life—baristas calling out orders, the clatter of plates and silverware, the hum of conversations. But in our small corner of the world, time had stopped.

"If you could do it over," Lucian said suddenly, his voice quieter, "would you still choose him?"

I parted my lips, but no words came out. Because I didn't have an answer. Finally, I admitted, "I don't know."

Lucian studied me for a long time before nodding. "At least that's honest."

I forced a small, sad smile. "I should go."

Lucian didn't stop me. He didn't reach for me or ask me to stay. He just watched as I slid my coat over my shoulders and stepped away from the table.

I made it to the door before his voice stopped me.

"Alina."

I turned, my heart hammering against my ribs.

Lucian's expression was unreadable, but his voice was softer this time. "Did he make you happy?"

The question hit me harder than I expected. My fingers tightened around the strap of my purse as I searched for an answer. I wanted to lie. I wanted to tell him that my choice was worth it. That the man I had chosen over him had been enough. But I couldn't. Because we both knew the truth.

I shook my head. "No."

Lucian nodded once, as if that was all he needed to hear. Then, without another word, he turned and walked away, leaving me standing there, drowning in the regret I had spent years trying to escape.

3 When we were everything

Love wasn't supposed to feel this easy. At least, that's what I told myself. Looking back, I don't know if it was love that made everything feel so light, or if it was simply the illusion of it—the way Lucian and I fit together so effortlessly, as if the universe had carved us from the same constellation. I recall the way he used to look at me, like I was the most beautiful thing he had ever seen, even when I was just sitting across from him, sipping coffee, rambling about something inconsequential. Those moments felt eternal. But eternity is a lie we tell ourselves when we're too afraid to face reality. I see that now.

Falling Without Fear

Falling in love wasn't supposed to feel like this—like something weightless, effortless, like slipping beneath warm water and letting it embrace you. For two people who had spent their lives fearing love, we somehow made it look easy. I remember the first time I realized I was falling for Lucian. It wasn't during some grand, cinematic moment. It was something small, almost unnoticeable—until it wasn't.

It was late, and we had just spent hours wandering the city, talking about everything and nothing. The air was crisp, the streets quiet, the world around us humming in the distance. We had stopped in front of my building, neither of us willing to say goodnight just yet. I had looked up at him, and for the first time, I wasn't scared. I wanted to fall.

Lucian had tucked a strand of hair behind my ear, his touch lingering for a second longer than necessary. "You're thinking too much again," he had murmured.

I smiled, shaking my head. "Maybe."

"You don't have to be afraid, Alina."

He had said it so simply, like it was the easiest truth in the world. And maybe, with him, it was.

Falling in love with Lucian had been like discovering a new language, one that only the two of us understood. It was in the way he traced patterns on my skin when he thought I was asleep. The way I found myself listening to songs he loved, just to feel closer to him when he wasn't around. The way we could sit in silence, and it never felt empty. I had spent so long running from love, convinced it was something fleeting, something dangerous. But with Lucian, I had wanted to stay. And maybe that's what scared me the most. Because when you fall without fear, you never think about the landing. And I never saw a crash coming.

"You're staring at me again," I teased, setting my mug down on the café table between us.

Lucian smirked, his fingers lazily tracing the rim of his own cup. "Can you blame me?"

I rolled my eyes, but I couldn't hide the warmth creeping up my neck. "Flattery isn't going to get you out of being late. Again."

He leaned forward, resting his arms on the table, the dim lighting casting shadows across his sharp features. "I got held up. You know how work gets."

I sighed, not because I was angry, but because I knew exactly what he was going to say before he even said it. That was the thing about us—our conversations had rhythms, patterns, like a song I had memorized long ago.

"Lucian, you work too much."

"And you worry too much."

"Because I care."

His smirk faltered, and for a moment, something unspoken passed between us. Something deeper than the words we so carefully danced around.

"I know you do," he said softly, reaching across the table, his fingers brushing against mine. "That's why I love you."

The world stopped. Or maybe it just slowed, just enough for me to feel the weight of those words settle between us.

I blinked. "What did you just say?"

Lucian smiled, tilting his head as if he had been waiting for this exact moment. "I love you, Alina."

I should have said it back right away. The words were there, on the tip of my tongue, waiting to be spoken into existence. But something inside me hesitated. Maybe it was fear. Maybe it was the quiet whisper in the back of my mind reminding me that nothing this perfect ever lasts.

The First I Love You

Later that night, as we lay tangled in his sheets, my head resting against his chest, I finally let myself say it.

"I love you too."

Lucian's fingers stopped tracing circles on my back, and he shifted slightly, his heartbeat steady beneath my cheek. "Say it again."

I smiled. "I love you."

His arms tightened around me. "One more time."

"Lucian, I love you."

He let out a soft breath, like he had been holding it in, afraid I might change my mind. "You have no idea how long I've waited to hear you say that."

I did, though. Because I had waited just as long to say it.

Perhaps love shouldn't have felt so effortless. Maybe that was the problem. Maybe when something feels too easy, you don't see the cracks forming beneath the surface. And by the time you do, it's already too late.

The First Cracks

There was a time when Lucian reached for my hand instinctively, when his lips brushed against my temple absentmindedly, when laughter came as easily as breathing. Then, slowly, the small things disappeared. First, the way he used to text me good morning. Then, the way he leaned into me when we walked together. The space between us became something I couldn't ignore.

"Do you still love me?" I whispered one evening as we lay in bed, both facing the ceiling, neither of us touching.

Lucian turned his head slightly, exhaling. "What kind of question is that?"

"An honest one."

Silence. And in that silence, I found my answer.

The Night Doubt Took Root

The first time I felt him slipping away, it wasn't loud. It wasn't a fight or a slammed door. Quietness fell between us. We sat on the couch, his phone lighting up between us. He glanced at it, turned it over, and exhaled as if the weight of something invisible had settled on his shoulders.

"Who was that?" I asked, my voice careful.

He hesitated. "Just work."

"You've been working a lot."

He nodded, his jaw tightening. "I know."

I wanted to push, to ask why his touch had become hesitant, why his laughter felt like an echo of what it once was. But I was afraid of the answer. And so, I let it go.

But doubt is a quiet intruder. It doesn't announce itself with fanfare or warnings. It seeps in through the cracks, making a home in the empty spaces where love used to live. The next few days felt different, though neither of us acknowledged it. Conversations became shorter. The space between us in bed stretched wider. He still kissed me goodbye before leaving in the morning, but it felt more like a habit than a desire.

One night, as I lay awake beside him, listening to the steady rhythm of his breathing, I reached for his hand beneath the sheets. He didn't pull away, but he also didn't hold on the way he used to. His fingers rested there—lifeless, unmoving—like they had forgotten how to want me. I stared at the ceiling, my heart beating in slow, painful thuds. Maybe I was overthinking it. Maybe I was imagining things. Maybe love changed, and I was just too scared to accept it. But deep down, I knew. Something between us had shifted, and there was no going back.

What We Lost

There was a time when his eyes softened when he looked at me, when my name on his lips sounded like something sacred. Now, there were more nights where we sat in silence, both of us too afraid to be the first to admit what we already knew—We were losing each other. Love, real love, wasn't about grand gestures. It wasn't about extravagant vacations or candlelit dinners. It was in the details, in the quiet moments, in the way he used to reach for my hand absentmindedly, in the way I used to listen to his breathing at night and feeling at peace. We had let those moments slip away. And by the time I noticed, it was already too late.

Goodbye Unspoken

Our ending was not a spectacle. No dramatic fight. No final, desperate plea. Just the slow realization that we were holding on to something that was already gone. He stopped reaching for me in the middle of the night. I stopped looking for him in the quiet spaces between conversations. And in the absence of love, doubt took its place. If only I had fought more fiercely. If only I had asked him to stay. But sometimes, the worst heartbreak isn't the one that shatters you all at once. It's the one that lets you break piece by piece, until there's nothing left to hold onto.

I remember the night we became strangers. We sat across from each other at the dinner table, two people who once shared the same heartbeat now struggling to find words to fill the silence. The food between us had gone cold, untouched.

4 The first lie

Some mistakes don't feel like mistakes when you make them. They feel small. Harmless. Like a stone dropped into a lake, barely making a ripple. But eventually, the ripples spread. They expand, they collide, and suddenly, what seemed insignificant becomes something unstoppable. And that's how it started—the first lie.

I remember the exact moment I told it. It wasn't planned. It wasn't carefully crafted. It just slipped out, so effortlessly that I almost believed it myself.

"Are you okay?" Lucian had asked, his brow furrowed, concerned.

I had been staring out the window, my mind elsewhere, my heart weighed down by something I wasn't ready to name. I could feel him watching me, waiting for an answer.

I should have told the truth. I should have let him in. But instead, I forced a smile and said, "I'm fine."

A simple lie. A small lie. But it was the first one.

Lies Don't Always Need Words

Lies don't always come in the form of words. Sometimes, they live in silence. In avoidance. In the things we don't say.

I told myself it didn't matter, that Lucian didn't need to know everything. That some things were better left unsaid. But the truth was, I was afraid. Afraid of how he would look at me if he knew what was really going on inside my head. Afraid he'd see me differently. Afraid he'd leave. So, I buried it. And the longer I buried it, the more distance it created between us. I was hiding the fact that I was scared that I was going to ruin everything. I was scared that I was going to push him away, just like I had with everyone else in my life. I feared my own patterns, and I was too afraid to change them.

Lucian's Suspicion

Lucian had always been the kind of person who paid attention to details. To patterns. And something about us was starting to feel off.

It started small. He noticed when I took longer than usual to answer my phone, when I smiled at a message but refused to tell him what it was about. He noticed when my schedule shifted, subtle changes that didn't seem to fit the way they once did. I stopped calling him on my breaks at work like I used to. The texts that once arrived throughout the day—small notes about what I was doing, what I was thinking—became less frequent, then stopped altogether. When he asked about it, I gave him vague answers, excusing it with being busy, distracted, tired.

Lucian never believed in blind faith. Trust, to him, was something earned, something carefully built. And now, something told him that whatever we had built was starting to crack.

So, he did what came naturally to him. He started investigating. It wasn't dramatic at first. He didn't follow me or search through my things. Instead, he watched. He listened. He paid attention to the things I didn't say, the gaps in my stories, the hesitation before I answered. Then he started testing me. A simple question asked twice in different ways, waiting to see if my answer changed. A casual mention of a place I said I had been, only for him to later ask what the weather had been like that day. Subtle things. Small things. But they were enough. Enough for him to realize something wasn't right. Enough for doubt to take root.

At first, he tried to push it aside. To reason with himself. Perhaps I was just distracted. Perhaps I was keeping things to myself for a reason that had nothing to do with deception. Perhaps he was overthinking it, letting his own insecurities cloud his judgment.

But trust isn't about perhaps. Trust is certainty. And certainty was slipping away from him like sand through his fingers. It was in the way my eyes flickered away just a second too quickly, how my excuses sounded rehearsed, how I no longer reached for him the way I used to.

Lucian began replaying moments, trying to make sense of the shift. He remembered how we used to be—how I once shared every little thing with him, how he never had to ask where I had been because I told him before he even though too. Now, there were missing pieces. And the more he looked, the more he realized those pieces weren't just misplaced. They were being deliberately hidden.

Lucian's Internal Battle

Lucian wasn't ready to confront me. Maybe it was because he needed to be sure. Or maybe it was because a part of him still wanted to believe in me, in us. He wasn't just looking for proof of a lie. He was searching for a reason not to believe it.

Because the person he knew me to be—the Alina he had built a life with—would never deceive him. And yet, the evidence kept building. The missing hours. The conversations cut short. The way my eyes darted away just a little too quickly when he asked the right questions.

Lucian wasn't just investigating me. He was trying to prove himself wrong. Trying to convince himself that I was still the person he thought I was. But with every day that passed, it became harder for him to ignore the truth he didn't want to face.

Late at night, he would lie awake, staring at the ceiling, wondering if he was imagining things. He would go over our conversations in his head, replaying moments, searching for something that could confirm his worst fears or silence them for good.

Some nights, he convinced himself he was paranoid. That love made people insecure, that perhaps he was reading too much into things. Perhaps I was just busy, distracted, stressed. He told himself that love wasn't always perfect, that relationships had ups and downs.

But other nights, the doubt clawed at him, relentless and unyielding. He found himself watching me more closely, noticing the hesitation in my voice, the way I avoided certain topics, the way my phone was always just out of his reach.

He hated himself for it. For suspicion. For the way he had started doubting the woman he had once trusted with everything. Lucian had always prided himself on being rational, logical. But love wasn't logical. It was messy and complicated and, sometimes, it was blind. And he had been blind to me for far too long.

Knowing Weight

Lucian had gathered enough pieces of the puzzle to see the picture forming in front of him. And it was a picture he didn't want to recognize. The late nights, the unexplained absences, the moments when I felt like a stranger even when I was right beside him.

He could have confronted me. He could have demanded answers. But he didn't. Because confronting me would mean admitting that the woman he had loved—the woman he still loved—was capable of deception. And that was something he couldn't bear to accept.

So he kept quiet. He waited. Hoping that, somehow, I would give him a reason to believe in me again. Hoping that perhaps, just perhaps, I would tell him the truth before he had to ask for it. But deep down, I think he already knew. I wasn't going to tell him. And he wasn't ready to hear it.

The Breaking Point

"Where were you today?" he asked one evening, his voice calm, careful.

"I told you. At work." I didn't flinch, didn't break eye contact. I had told this lie enough times that it felt natural.

Lucian nodded slowly. "I called your office. They said you left early."

My breath caught for just a second—just long enough for him to notice.

"I—I had an errand to run," I said quickly, forcing a casual shrug. "It wasn't a big deal."

He didn't say anything at first. Just watched me. I studied.

"Okay," he finally said. "I believe you."

But that was another lie. Because I saw it in his eyes. Lucian didn't believe me at all. And I had just given him every reason to keep looking for the truth. The only problem? Once he found it, I wasn't sure if I'd ever be able to take it back.

The Moment of No Return

Lucian stayed up that night, staring at the ceiling, feeling the weight of something irreversible settle in his chest. The realization had been creeping in for weeks' small details that didn't add up, silences that stretched too long, the quiet unraveling of life he thought was unshakable. But now, the truth wasn't creeping anymore. It was knocking. Loud. Insistent.

He turned onto his side, staring at the empty space beside him. Alina was asleep, her breathing slow and steady. Peaceful. Or maybe just pretending to be. He wondered if she had always been this good at lying, or if she had learned along the way. If the woman he had fallen for had ever really existed, or if she had been slipping through his fingers long before he noticed.

His chest tightened as he thought back to the early days, to the way she used to call him between every break at work, her voice filled with stories of mundane things, things that didn't matter but somehow made him feel like he mattered to her. Now, there were no calls. No texts.

But trust wasn't about maybe.

And in his heart, Lucian already knew.

He was past the point of return.

There was no fixing this.

Only waiting for the moment, it all shattered.

Lucian stayed up that night, staring at the ceiling, realizing that the foundation of everything he had built with me was beginning to crack.

He wasn't ready to confront me.

But he knew—deep down—that the truth was coming.

And once it did, nothing would ever be the same again.

5 The first cracks

Love doesn't shatter all at once. It cracks first. Slowly. Subtly. Like a hairline fracture in glass, barely visible at first. But then, pressure builds. Tension spreads. And before you know it, everything collapses. That's how it was with us. The moment I lied to Lucian, I set something in motion. And now, piece by piece, we were breaking.

The Silence That Said Everything

Lucian didn't confront me right away. He let the silence do the talking. At first, I thought I had gotten away with it. That he believed me. That our world was still intact. But I should have known better. Lucian was never the type to let things go. He noticed the inconsistencies, the hesitation in my voice, the way I held my breath for just a second too long before answering his questions. He was watching me now, always watching. And I felt it. The weight of his silence pressed against me like an unseen force, heavy and suffocating. He hadn't accused me of anything outright, but his eyes—God, his eyes—they held doubt. At night, when we lay in bed, the quiet between us grew into chasm. I could feel the questions hanging in the air, unspoken but deafening. "Alina," he murmured once, just as I was drifting off. His voice was quiet, but there was something sharp beneath it. I pretended to be asleep. Because I knew if I opened my mouth, I would have to lie again. And I was already drowning in them.

The Space Between Us

His habits changed; he was distant. He stopped asking where I had been and ceased texting me during the day. Instead of relief, a heavy dread settled over me. His silence felt calculated, a test. A way to see if I would confess without prompting. I remained silent. The tension was a physical thing, stretching across the bed at night, settling between our bodies like an unspoken war. I wanted to reach for him; to tell him I missed us. But I was afraid of what I would find in his eyes. Mornings that used to start with sleepy smiles and whispered greetings became rushed and mechanical. He no longer kissed my forehead before leaving for work or asked if I wanted to meet for lunch. When I came home late, he barely acknowledged it. We sat at opposite ends of the couch in the evenings, each pretending to be absorbed in our own world. One night, I reached for his hand. He let it rest there before placing as much space as possible between us. He also stopped waiting for me to come home before eating dinner. These weren't conscious decisions, just changes. Small, almost imperceptible shifts that added up to something undeniable. The love we once had wasn't disappearing all at once. It was fading, slowly, painfully, moment by moment. And the worst part? I was letting it.

Lucian's Restless Nights

His nights were tormented. I could hear him shifting in bed, his breathing uneven, his body tense beside me. He stared at me as if searching for answers. I withheld the truth. He retreated to his office, staying up late. One night, I woke to find him sitting on the edge of the bed, staring at his hands. "Lucian," I whispered, reaching out. He flinched. And I knew then—we weren't just breaking. We were already broke.

The Weight of Sleepless Nights

The next night, his nights were just as rough. He would lie awake for hours, his breathing shallow, his body stiff beside mine. I could feel the tension radiating off him. Then one night, he left the bed altogether. I heard him pacing in the living room, the soft creak of the floorboards beneath his steps. The sound of ice clinking in a glass. The faint flicker of a lighter. Lucian didn't smoke anymore. Except for now, he did. Except now, something inside him was unraveling so fast, he needed something to steady himself. I wanted to go to him. But the words never came. Instead, I stayed in bed, listening to the quiet sounds of a man losing himself in the dark. By the time he returned to bed, the scent of smoke lingered, mixing with something like regret.

The First Real Argument

It happened over something small. A misplaced phone. A question I dodged one too many times. "Where the hell were you last night,

Alina?" Lucian's voice was low, controlled, but there was something simmering beneath it. I froze. "I told you. I had a late meeting." His jaw clenched. "No, you didn't. I called your office. You weren't there." My stomach dropped. "Lucian, it's not what you think." "Then tell me what it is. Tell me why you keep lying to me." His voice cracked, and it hurt. I could have told him then, but I didn't. "You're being paranoid," I muttered. A bitter laugh left his lips. "Am I? Then tell me why you won't look at me when you say that." I didn't answer. And that was the moment I knew—we weren't just cracking anymore. We were breaking.

The Tipping Point

The worst part wasn't the argument, it was the moment he stopped fighting. Lucian ran a hand through his hair, exhaling shakily. "I don't know who you are anymore, Alina." His words should have stung, but all I felt was exhaustion. "I keep trying to make sense of it," he muttered. "The truth is you made a choice. And it wasn't me." His voice was steadier now. "I loved you, Alina," he said quietly. "I loved you even when I knew I shouldn't. Even when I started seeing the cracks. Even when I realized I was the only one holding on." He took a deep breath. "But I'm donc chasing after something that doesn't want to be caught." The finality in his voice made my stomach twist. He was just…done. And for the first time, I understood what true loss felt like.

6 The secret she never told him

Secrets have weight. They press against the heart, filling the empty spaces between unspoken words. They create distance even in the closest connections, casting shadows on shared moments and building invisible walls between hearts that once beat in sync.

She never told him the truth—not because she wanted to deceive him, but because she feared the words would shatter their fragile balance. It wasn't betrayal, nor a grand revelation. It was a simple, buried truth: she didn't believe she deserved him.

Not because he was imperfect, but because she had convinced herself love was earned. Her past mistakes, insecurities, and fears whispered she wasn't enough. She pushed him away, built walls of silence, and let doubt dictate her choices. She never voiced her love in ways he needed. She believed her presence was enough, but love requires affirmation, words that bridge gaps and mend cracks.

Now, it was too late. The silence had grown too heavy, the distance too wide. The love they shared was a ghost. The secret was that she never learned to love herself enough to believe his love was real. Her self-doubt drove them apart.

The Ghosts of What Once Was

Surrounded by remnants of their shared past, she felt the ghosts of what could have been. Every place, every memory, haunted her. She saw his boyish charm, remembered the warmth of his touch, the way he looked at her as if she were the world. Now, his eyes held hurt and confusion. He didn't understand her withdrawal, the secret that had eaten her away. It was too late to explain.

The Walls She Built

In solitude, she reflected on the walls she had built fear as bricks, doubt as cement. They hadn't protected her, but trapped her in insecurity, preventing true connection. She had focused on self-preservation, blind to the damage she caused. Those walls were manifestations of past pain, voices telling her she wasn't enough. In trying to shield herself, she had caused the very pain she feared.

Standing amidst the ruins, she felt profound sorrow. She had been her own enemy, allowing fear to dictate her life.

A Journey to Self-Acceptance

She knew the only way forward was self-acceptance. She needed to confront her demons, dismantle those walls, and embrace her worth. This wouldn't be easy. She would face her fears, challenge her lies, and learn to love herself.

One afternoon, sitting in their favorite cafe alone, she remembered Lucian's patient gaze. He had always seen her worth, even when she couldn't. She realized that vulnerability was strength, a way to reclaim her narrative. She began to dismantle the walls, brick by brick, freeing herself from the weight of her past.

She sought solace in reflection, allowing herself to feel the buried pain. She reached out to friends, finding strength in their words. Slowly, she learned to forgive herself, to let go of guilt and shame. She embraced her humanity, understanding imperfection was part of life, and that she was worthy of love.

Looking to the future, she felt a glimmer of hope. One day, she would find the strength to love and be loved, free from secrets and doubts. She was ready to embrace her worth, to believe in herself, and to open her heart to the possibilities of what could be.

7 The moment I found out

The truth doesn't always come with a crash. Sometimes, it slips in quietly, a subtle shift settling into the spaces between suspicion and certainty. It wasn't a single moment that unraveled everything—it was a series of them, each adding weight to the realization that something had fundamentally changed.

I had known, deep down, before the proof ever reached my hands. I knew in the way his voice lacked its usual warmth when he spoke my name. In the way his eyes flickered away, a silent confession. In the way his touch felt like a faded photograph, a distant memory of what used to be.

But knowing and accepting are worlds apart. And for a while, I existed in that painful limbo.

The Unraveling

I found out in the quietest way—not through a dramatic confrontation, but through the absence of what should have been. The missing pieces of our routine, the unanswered calls, the moments claimed by another.

The way love fades is slow, insidious unraveling. A series of small betrayals that, when pieced together, form a truth too agonizing to ignore. I remembered the first whisper of doubt; the first time I felt a cold dread settle in my chest. It wasn't the forgotten goodnight text or the flimsy excuses; it was the way he stopped reaching for me in the quiet moments we once shared.

Love Makes You Blind

Love makes you blind, they say. But I wasn't blind. I saw the signs. I felt the shift before I could name it. Yet, I clung to the belief in her. Until that moment I couldn't anymore.

She thought I didn’t notice her withdrawal. The way she stopped calling during work. The way her touch became a feather-light graze, as if afraid I’d feel the guilt seeping from her skin.

Then, I found out. And it wasn’t just the betrayal that shattered me. It was the look in her eyes afterward—like I was merely collateral damage in her internal war.

"Do you remember when I asked if I could kiss you?" I asked, my voice barely whispered.

Alina flinched, but didn’t look away.

I waited, but she didn’t answer. Perhaps she was searching for nonexistent words.

"You should have stopped me," I said, a bitter edge to my tone.

Her lips parted, and in a small voice, she admitted, "I wanted to kiss you too, so I couldn’t ask you to stop."

A hollow chuckle escaped me. "That’s the problem, Alina. You always do what you want, without thinking about what it destroys."

She remained silent, acknowledging the truth.

Confrontation

The confrontation was inevitable. I had seen the text messages, the words of affection meant for another. A cold dread settled in my chest.

"It's him or me," I said, my voice cracking. "You have to choose."

She hesitated, her eyes darting between her phone and me. The silence was a heavy blanket, suffocating.

"I chose him," she whispered, her voice barely audible.

The ground shifted beneath me. "Why?" I demanded, my voice hoarse.

She looked up, tears streaming down her face. "Because of circumstances," she said, her voice trembling. "Because I felt unloved. Because I thought you were always in love with your ex. Because I was scared I was going to lose you, and he was there. Because I felt alone."

"And the last reason?" I asked, my voice barely whispered.

She closed her eyes. "Because I love him so much," she admitted.

The Breaking Point

The hardest part wasn't the betrayal itself. It was the realization that she had been clinging to a ghost fighting for love that had already abandoned her. I had been searching her eyes for something that no longer existed.

She wanted to ask why, to tell the truth. But she didn't need to. The truth wasn't in my words; it was in my silence. In the way I didn't fight for her, didn't reach for her as she walked away. In the way I let her go, as if she had never truly belonged.

The Moment She Chose Herself

She thought knowing would break her. She thought the truth would shatter her.

But it did something else. It set her free.

She deserved more than unanswered questions and half-truths. She deserved more than love that made her doubt her worth. She deserved someone who knew how to hold on.

And at that moment, she found herself. She chose her own heart.

The Aftermath of Discovery

The days that followed were a blur. I cycled between anger, sadness, and confusion. The world moved in slow motion. My friends offered comfort, but they didn't understand the depth of the wound.

I replied to our last conversations, searching for missed clues. The silence between his words was deafening, filled with hidden meanings. Every pause, every hesitation, was a telltale sign.

I realized his silence was a way to avoid confrontation, to keep me at arm's length. It allowed the distance to grow, to fester. Now, it was a chasm.

A New Beginning

Amidst the pain, I saw a glimmer of a new beginning. The discovery shattered my illusions but gave me clarity. I deserved more than half-hearted love.

I began to rebuild, finding strength in my resilience. I sought new experiences, embraced new passions, and allowed myself to dream again. My worth wasn't defined by his love or betrayal, but by my own.

Standing on the precipice of a new chapter, I felt hope. I was ready to face the road ahead with purpose and determination. I had found myself in heartbreak, and now I was ready to embrace the journey.

8 The night I knew he knew

Some truths don't need to be spoken. You can feel them in silence.

And that night, in the silence between us, I knew he knew.

"Sorry for what comes next," Lucian murmured, his voice like steel wrapped in quiet devastation.

He wasn't going to scream. He wasn't going to rage. No, that would've been too easy. Too human.

Instead, he was going to do what would hurt the most.

"I wanted to hate you," he continued, his gaze locked onto mine. "I wanted to let the anger swallow me whole, to turn my pain into something sharp, something that could cut you the way you cut me."

A breath hitched my throat, but he didn't stop.

"But I can't." His voice was almost gentle now, and that was the cruelest part.

"So instead, I'll do the only thing left. Since I can't hate you, I'll make you hate me. I'll be the villain in your story, the storm you never saw coming. Not because I want revenge—but because it's the only way to break free."

My hands trembled at my sides. "Lucian"

"Maybe if you hate me, you'll finally have a purpose. A reason to justify what you've done." His lips twitched into something that wasn't quite a smile. "And maybe then, I'll finally let go too."

Tears burned behind my eyes. "I can't stand you hating me. I can't bear to watch you humiliate me. I can't bear to see you change with me—just as I can't bear to lose you."

Lucian exhaled slowly, as if he had already made peace with this. "You should've thought about that before you threw us away."

Confrontation

The confrontation was inevitable. He had seen the text messages on her phone, the words of affection and longing meant for someone else. He felt a cold, hard lump form in his chest as he read them, the reality of her betrayal sinking in.

"It's him or me," he said, his voice breaking with the weight of the ultimatum. "You have to choose."

She hesitated, her eyes darting between the phone and him. The silence stretched on, each second a knife twisting deeper into his heart.

"I chose him," she whispered, her voice barely audible.

He felt the ground shift beneath him, a wave of nausea washing over him as the truth solidified. "Why?" he demanded, his voice hoarse.

She looked at him with tear-filled eyes. "Because of circumstances," she said, her voice trembling. "Because I felt unloved. Because I thought you were always in love with your ex."

He shook his head, disbelief etched across his face. "And the last reason?" he asked, his voice barely whispered.

She closed her eyes, tears streaming down her face. "Because I love him so much," she admitted.

Goodbye Unspoken

He did not accuse her.

He did not demand answers.

He did not need to.

The night he knew, he simply looked at her in a way he never had before—with sorrow, with understanding, with the kind of quiet devastation that does not ask for an explanation.

And she knew, then, that they had already lost each other.

There was no need for a fight, no need for raised voices or shattered words. The love they once held had already slipped through their fingers, leaving behind only the echo of something that had once been real.

The Moment She Saw the Truth

For so long, she had convinced herself that love could survive anything. That if she stayed, if she tried harder, if she pretended well enough, they could find their way back to what they once were.

But in that moment, with his gaze heavy upon her, she understood.

This was not love anymore.

This was grief.

And the hardest thing she would ever have to do was let it go.

The Aftermath of Realization

As the days turned into weeks, she found herself replaying that moment in her mind repeatedly. The way he had looked at her, the sorrow in his eyes, the unspoken goodbye that had passed between them. It haunted her, a constant reminder of her own failings, of the love she had lost.

She could see the change in him, the way he had become more distant, more guarded. He no longer reached for her in the middle of the night, no longer whispered sweet nothings in her ear. The love they had shared had become a distant memory, overshadowed by the weight of her guilt and the reality of their new normal.

The Struggle to Move On

Moving on felt impossible. Every corner of their home was filled with memories of what once was. The laughter that had echoed through their halls, the tender moments they had shared, the promises they had made to each other. It all felt like a cruel reminder of what she had lost.

She struggled to find a way forward, to reconcile the love she still felt for him with the reality of their fractured relationship. She wanted to hold on, to fight for what they once had, but she knew that it was a battle she couldn't win alone. The love they had shared had been built on trust, and that trust had been irrevocably broken.

Finding Redemption

During her sorrow, she began to search for redemption. She sought solace in the quiet moments of reflection, in the words of those who had walked a similar path. She realized that she needed to forgive herself before she could ever hope to find forgiveness from him.

She began to work on herself, to confront the insecurities and fears that had driven her actions. She sought therapy, found new hobbies, and began to rebuild her sense of self-worth. It was a long and difficult journey, but with each passing day, she felt a small sense of progress.

The Hope for Reconciliation

While she knew that their love could never return to what it once was, she held onto a small glimmer of hope. Hope that, in time, they can find a way to heal, to build a new relationship based on honesty and understanding. She knew it wouldn't be easy, and that the road ahead would be filled with challenges, but she was willing to try.

She understood now that love required more than just staying; it required growth, vulnerability, and a willingness to confront the darkest parts of oneself. And as she looked towards the future, she felt a sense of determination to become the person she had always wanted to be, both for herself and for him.

9 The night I gave one last chance

I knew I shouldn't have. I knew I was setting myself up for more pain. But some part of me—maybe the part that still ached for her—needed to see if there was anything left worth saving.

One last chance. That's what I told myself.

But in the end, it wasn't about second chances. It was about realizing that love, no matter how deep, can't survive without trust.

She stood in front of me, her eyes wide with something I couldn't name—hope? Fear? Guilt? Maybe all three.

"Lucian," she whispered. "Please."

I wanted to believe her. God, I wanted to believe her so badly. But the past was a weight I couldn't shake.

"Tell me the truth," I said, hoarse voice. "Did you ever really love me? Or was I just another choice you got wrong?"

Her breath caught, and in that moment, I saw the answer in her eyes before she even spoke.

And that was the moment I knew—I couldn't give her another chance. Because she had already used them all.

The Lingering Doubt

As I stared at her, memories of our time together flooded my mind. The laughter, the tears, the quiet moments we had shared. Each memory was tainted now, overshadowed by the betrayal that had shattered our trust. I wanted to find a way back to what we once had, but I knew that path no longer existed.

"I never meant to hurt you," she said, her voice trembling. "I just... I didn't know how to handle everything. I was lost."

Her words hung in the air, a fragile attempt at an explanation. But they did little to soothe the ache in my heart. I had heard it all before—the excuses, the justifications. They were empty now, devoid of meaning.

"You think that makes it better?" I asked, bitterness lacing my words. "You think saying you were lost somehow erases the pain you caused?"

She shook her head, tears spilling down her cheeks. "No, I know it doesn't. But I'm willing to do whatever it takes to make it right."

The Offer of Redemption

A part of me wanted to believe her, to take her at her word and give her the chance to prove herself. But the wounds were still fresh, and the scars ran too deep. Trust was a fragile thing, and once broken, it was nearly impossible to mend.

"And what if I can't?" I asked, my voice barely above a whisper. "What if I can't ever trust you again?"

She took a step closer, her eyes pleading. "Then let me show you. Let me earn your trust back. Just give me the chance to make things right."

I looked into her eyes, searching for any sign of deceit. But all I saw was desperation, a yearning for redemption that mirrored my own desire for closure.

"Why him?" I asked, my voice cracking. "Why did you choose him over me?"

She looked down, unable to meet my gaze. "It wasn't about him. It was about me. I felt unloved, unworthy. I thought you were still in love with your ex, and I convinced myself that I needed something else. Something more."

The Final Decision

Her words cut deep, but they also revealed the truth I had been avoiding. Our relationship had been built on a foundation of insecurity and doubt, and that foundation had crumbled under the weight of our own fears.

"I wanted to hate you," I said, my voice trembling. "I wanted to let the anger swallow me whole, to turn my pain into something sharp, something that could cut you the way you cut me."

She looked up, her eyes wide with fear. "Lucian, please..."

"But I can't," I continued, my voice breaking. "So instead, I'll do the only thing left. Since I can't hate you, I'll make you hate me. I'll be the villain in your story, the storm you never saw coming. Not because I want revenge—but because it's the only way to break free."

Her hands trembled at her sides, tears streaming down her face. "I can't stand you hating me. I can't bear to watch you humiliate me. I can't bear to see you change with me—just as I can't bear to lose you."

Lucian exhaled slowly, as if he had already made peace with this. "You should've thought about that before you threw us away."

The Plea for Redemption

"Promise me one thing," I pleaded, my voice cracking. "Don't go back to your old life. Don't become the man who fills his emptiness with meaningless faces, the man who let's love slip through his fingers like it was never real."

His jaw tightened. "Why do you care?"

I swallowed hard. "Because I was proud when you told me you changed. When you said you were tempted, that you were asked—but still, you refused. That meant something to me. It still does."

A flicker of something crossed his face, but it was gone before I could name it.

"So please… Even if you hate me, even if I no longer have a place in your life—don't become that man again." My voice wavered. "Not like my second boyfriend."

Lucian's expression hardened at that, and for a moment, I thought he might say something—anything.

But he didn't.

Instead, he just turned and walked away.

The Aftermath

As he walked away, I felt a mix of emotions, relief, sorrow, and a lingering sense of emptiness. I had hoped for redemption, for a chance to make things right. But I knew now that some wounds were too deep to heal, some betrayals too profound to forgive.

I stood there, alone in silence, the weight of my choices pressing down on me. The love we had shared was gone, replaced by a chasm of mistrust and regret. And at that moment, I realized that the only way to move forward was to let go.

I took a deep breath, wiping away the tears that had fallen. It was time to start anew, to find a way to rebuild myself and my life. I couldn't change the past, but I could learn from it. And with that knowledge, I would find the strength to move on.

10 The wrong man

Regret is the cruelest teacher. It comes too late, whispering lessons you should have learned before you lose everything.

I stood there, drowning in it, as I looked at Lucian.

"I made a mistake," I finally admitted, my voice barely above a whisper.

He didn't flinch. He didn't react. It was like my words bounced off the walls he had built between us.

"I chose wrong," I continued, swallowing back the lump in my throat. "I thought Alex Deblozay could offer me something you couldn't. I thought he was the safe choice, the rational one. But I was wrong."

Lucian's eyes darkened, but he remained silent.

"Alex was everything you weren't. Steady. Predictable. He never challenged me, never made me feel like I had something to lose," I whispered. "But maybe that was the problem."

Lucian's jaw clenched. "And now what do you expect? Redemption? Forgiveness?"

I shook my head. "No. I just need you to know—I never stopped loving you. Even when I convinced myself I did. Even when I tried to replace you."

Lucian's gaze was unreadable. "You made your choice, Alina. Now you have to live with it."

And just like that, the weight of my decision crushed me.

The Depth of Regret

Regret has a way of seeping into every corner of your mind, coloring every memory with shades of what could have been. As I stood there, facing the man I had wronged, I felt the full weight of my choices pressing down on me.

"I thought I was making the right decision," I said, my voice barely above a whisper. "I thought I was choosing stability, security. But in doing so, I lost the one thing that truly mattered—us."

Lucian's expression remained unreadable, but I could see the pain flicker in his eyes. It was a pain I had caused, and the knowledge of that cut deeper than any words ever could.

"Alex was safe," I continued, my voice trembling. "He was the easy choice. But he was also the wrong one. He never made me feel the way you did. He never made me feel alive."

The Confession

Lucian's silence was a heavy, suffocating presence. I wanted him to say something, anything, to give me a sign that there was still a chance for redemption. But I knew that was a foolish hope.

"I don't expect you to forgive me," I said, my voice breaking. "I know I don't deserve it. But I need you to know that I'm sorry. I'm sorry for everything."

His gaze hardened, and for a moment, I thought he might walk away. But then he spoke, his voice low and filled with a quiet intensity.

"Sorry doesn't change what you did," he said. "It doesn't erase the betrayal, the hurt. You made your choice, Alina. And now you have to live with the consequences."

The Weight of Reality

His words hit me like a physical blow, but I knew they were true. I had made my choice, and now I had to face the reality of it. There was no going back, no undoing the past. All I could do was try to move forward, to find a way to live with the regret that haunted me.

"I understand," I whispered, tears streaming down my face. "I just... I needed you to know. I needed you to hear it from me."

Lucian's gaze softened for a brief moment, and I saw a flicker of the man I had once loved. But it was fleeting, and the walls between us remained.

"I appreciate your honesty," he said, his voice cold but not unkind. "But it doesn't change anything. We're done, Alina. This is the end."

The End of an Era

As he turned to walk away, I felt a sense of finality settle over me. This was the end of an era, the end of a love that had once been everything to me. I had made my choice, and now I had to live with the consequences.

"Goodbye, Lucian," I whispered, my voice choked with emotion. "I'll always love you."

He paused for a moment, as if considering his response. Then he simply nodded and walked away, leaving me standing alone with my regret.

The Path to Redemption

In the days that followed, I struggled to come to terms with my decision. The regret was a constant companion, a reminder of the love I had lost. But I knew I couldn't let it consume me. I had to find a way to move forward, to build a new life for myself.

I sought out therapy, trying to understand the choices I had made and the reasons behind them. I reached out to friends and family, finding solace in their support and understanding. And slowly, I began to rebuild my sense of self-worth, to find a way to forgive myself for the mistakes I had made.

Hope for the Future

As time passed, I began to see glimmers of hope on the horizon. I found new passions, new dreams, and new relationships. I learned to trust again, to open my heart to the possibility of love. And while the pain of losing Lucian never fully disappeared, I found a way to carry it with me, a reminder of the lessons I had learned.

I knew that I would always carry a part of him with me, that the love we had shared would always be a part of my story. But I also knew that I had the strength to move forward, to build a new life for myself. And with that knowledge, I took the first steps towards a brighter future.

The Darkness of the Night

But the nights were the hardest.

In the quiet darkness, when there was no distraction to occupy my mind, the weight of my regret became unbearable. I lay awake, staring at the ceiling, replying every moment, every decision, every mistake that had led to this point.

"Why did I choose him?" I whispered to myself, the question echoing in silence. **"Why did I throw away everything we had for someone who never made me feel the way you did?"**

The darkness offered no answers, only the cold, unyielding truth of my actions. I had chosen wrong, and now I had to live with that choice. But the regret, the sadness, the longing for what could have been—it consumed me.

The Ghost of Lucian

Everywhere I looked, I saw Lucian. His smile, his laughter, the way his eyes lit up when he saw me. The memories haunted me, a constant reminder of what I had lost.

"I'm sorry," I whispered into the empty room, tears streaming down my face. **"I'm so sorry."**

But the words felt hollow, empty. There was no one to hear them, no one to offer forgiveness or solace. I was alone, left to navigate the depths of my own sorrow.

The Longing for Redemption

I longed for redemption, for a chance to make things right. But I knew that some wounds were too deep to heal, some mistakes too profound to forgive. I had to find a way to live with my choices, to find a path forward despite the weight of my regret.

I clung to the hope that one day, I would find peace. That I would be able to look back on this time with understanding, with acceptance. But for now, I was lost in the darkness, searching for a way out.

The Glimmer of Hope

And then, in the midst of the darkness, a glimmer of hope appeared. It was faint, barely visible, but it was enough to keep me going.

I knew that the path to redemption would be long and difficult, but I was determined to find it. I would learn from my mistakes, I would become a better person, and I would find a way to move forward.

And with that glimmer of hope, I took the first steps towards a brighter future.

11 WHEN I DECIDED TO MAKE HER HATE ME

Love doesn't just disappear. It rots. And if I had to carry this decay inside me, so would she.

I was done waiting for the pain to fade. If I couldn't have peace, neither could she.

So, I made my choice. I would become the man she could never forgive.

I didn't want revenge. I wanted to release it. I wanted to sever the last string that tied me to her, even if it meant setting fire to everything we had left.

So, I became cruel. Deliberate. Every word, every look, every moment was calculated to break her.

She thought she knew me. She thought she understood my silence, my anger, my grief.

But this was a side of me she had never met before.

I let her see me with other women, let her believe I had moved on faster than she could blink. I let her hear the rumors, the ones I didn't bother denying. I let her feel the weight of being discarded, the way she once discarded me.

And when she finally broke, when she finally looked at me with something worse than regret—with hatred, I knew I had won.

Or at least, I should have. Because if I had truly won… Then why did it still hurt?

The Decay of Love

Love doesn't vanish overnight. It decays, leaving behind a bitter residue of what once was. Every memory, every shared moment now twisted with pain. And as that decay spread within me, I knew it would consume her too. She needed to understand the depths of my anguish, the silent torment that gnawed at my soul.

"If I have to live with this rot, so will she," I muttered to myself, feeling the resolve harden within me. **"I won't be the only one carrying this burden."**

So, I made my choice. I would transform into the man she could never forgive.

The Strategy

It wasn't about revenge. It was about release. I needed to sever the last string that tied me to her, even if it meant setting fire to everything we had left. I meticulously crafted my actions, each one designed to drive her further away, to make her detest me.

I became cruel. Deliberate. Every word, every look, every moment was calculated to break her. She thought she understood my silence, my anger, my grief—but this was a side of me she had never met before.

"You wanted a villain, Alina," I whispered as I watched her from afar. **"Well, here he is."**

The Painful Performance

I let her see me with other women, let her believe I had moved on faster than she could blink. I let her hear the rumors, the ones I didn't bother denying. I wanted her to feel the weight of being discarded, the way she once discarded me.

"Lucian, who's she?" she had asked once, her voice tinged with desperation.

"None of your business," I had replied coldly, watching as the pain flickered in her eyes.

Each calculated move was a dagger to her heart, but it was also a dagger to my own. Because in hurting her, I was hurting myself. Each step I took down this path only deepened the chasm between us, but it also deepened the wound within me.

The Moment of Realization

And then it happened. She finally broke. Her eyes, once filled with love and regret, now burned with hatred. She looked at me as if I was the monster I had become, and in that moment, I should have felt triumph.

But instead, I felt hollow.

"I hate you," she had said, her voice trembling with emotion. "I wish I had never met you."

Those words should have been a victory, the final nail in the coffin of our shattered relationship. But they weren't. They echoed in the empty spaces of my heart, amplifying the pain instead of dulling it.

The Unanswered Questions

If I had truly won, then why did it still hurt? Why did her hatred, instead of setting me free, feel like another chain binding me to the past? I had wanted release, but all I found was another layer of agony.

"Maybe I never wanted to be free," I whispered to myself, staring into the void. **"Maybe I just wanted her to feel my pain."**

In my quest to make her hate me, I had only succeeded in deepening my own wounds. Love, twisted and decayed, had turned into a weapon I couldn't control.

"Love doesn't just disappear," I repeated, feeling the weight of my own words. **"It rots. And now, we're both decaying."**

The Empty Victory

The realization was a bitter pill to swallow. I had set out to break her, to make her hate me, but in the end, I had only broken myself. The victory I sought was hollow, a fleeting moment of satisfaction that quickly dissolved into more pain.

"What have I done?" I asked myself, the enormity of my actions crashing down on me. **"What have I become?"**

I had turned into a villain, not just in her story, but in my own. And as I stood there, engulfed in the ruins of what we once had, I understood that there was no going back. The path I had chosen had led us both to this point, and now we are both trapped in the decay of our broken love.

The Final Thought

As I walked away from the scene of my own destruction, I couldn't help but wonder if there was a way out. A way to heal, to find redemption. But for now, the pain was too raw, too overwhelming. All I could do was carry the weight of my choices, hoping that one day, I would find a way to live with the man I had become.

"If this is what love does," I thought, staring into the night, **"then maybe it's better to let it rot."**

But deep down, I knew that love, even in its decay, was still a part of me. And that was the cruelest lesson of all.

I had spent so much time trying to understand his cruelty, searching for meaning in the way he had twisted the knife. But some things don't come with explanations. Some pain isn't meant to be rationalized, only survived.

Lucian had set fire to everything between us, hoping the ashes would bury me. But I refused to disappear beneath the weight of his anger.

I would not be his collateral damage.

And that was the moment I knew—I had to save myself.

12 Becoming whole again

Healing is not just about surviving the storm. It is about learning to dance in the rain, to lift your face toward the sky and let the water wash over you without fear. It is about understanding that pain does not make you unworthy of love, that brokenness does not mean you are beyond repair. Healing is the quiet unraveling of grief, the slow transformation of wounds into wisdom. It is the gentle act of releasing what no longer serves you, of loosening your grip on a past that once felt like the only thing tethering you to existence. It is the realization that time does not erase pain, but it softens its edges, turning sharp agony into something bearable, something that no longer cuts you open at every mention of a name, every whisper of a memory. Healing is about rediscovering the parts of yourself that you abandoned while loving someone else. It is about breathing deeply again without fearing the silence that follows. It is about filling the spaces within you with your own presence, your own joy, your own voice. I once thought that healing meant returning to who I used to be, but now I see that is not the goal. Healing is not about going back. It is about becoming someone new, someone who carries the past not as a burden, but as a testament to resilience. And I was finally ready to step into that version of myself.

Letting Go Without Losing

Moving on does not mean I have to forget. I used to think that in order to truly heal, I had to erase him, had to push every memory of him into the deepest corners of my mind. But love—real love—does not disappear just because it is no longer present. It lingers in the spaces we once occupied, in the lessons it left behind, in the way it shaped me. So, I do not force myself to forget. Instead, I let go with grace. I allow the memories to exist without anchoring me to the past. I let them be part of my story, not the thing that defines it. Love does not have to be permanent to be meaningful. It does not have to last forever to have mattered. I release the weight of what could have been. And I hold onto the gratitude for what it was. Letting go to is not severing; it is learning to carry something differently. It is the quiet understanding that what once held my heart will always remain a part of me, but it no longer needs to dictate my every breath. It is the freedom of knowing that love does not always end with destruction, it can end with appreciation, with growth, with acceptance. There are moments when the past still reaches for me, whispering my name in familiar places, lingers in the scent of an old book or the melody of a forgotten song. But I do not flinch. I do not run. I let it exist alongside me, knowing that its presence does not diminish the life I am building now. Because letting go does not mean losing. It means making space for something new.

Reclaiming My Own Reflection

For the longest time, I saw myself through his eyes. I measured my worth by the way he loved me, by the way he looked at me. But standing here now, I realize that my worth was never something for someone else to define. So, I look in the mirror, and I see myself for who I am—not through the lens of someone else's love, but through my own eyes. I see a woman who has known loss and survived it. A woman who has known love and learned from it. A woman who has fallen apart and rebuilt herself piece by piece. I no longer search for validation in someone else's gaze. I am enough on my own. But relearning how to see myself was not easy. It took time. It took standing in front of the mirror, searching for the person I had once been, and realizing she was never lost—she was just waiting for me to return to her. I traced the outlines of my face, the same face he once traced with his fingertips, but this time I did not wonder how he had seen me. I did not seek approval in the reflection. Instead, I looked deeper, into my own eyes, into the depths of the person I was becoming. For so long, I had let love define me—let it tell me who I was, let it dictate my worth. But love, when it is true, does not complete you. It does not fill the empty spaces; it simply walks beside you as you learn to fill them yourself. I see myself now—not as someone waiting to be chosen, not as someone hoping to be seen, but as someone who chooses herself, as someone who sees herself fully and without hesitation. And that is enough.

A New Kind of Love

Maybe one day, love will find me again. But it will not be the desperate kind of love, the kind that clings, the kind that fears loss more than it embraces presence. It will be love that feels like coming home, not like searching for missing pieces. A love that stands on solid ground, that does not ask me to be anything other than who I am. But until then, I will love myself in all the ways I once wished someone else would. I will show up for myself. I will hold space for my own dreams, my own joy, my own quiet moments of peace. I will be my own greatest love story. Love, I have come to understand, is not something you chase. It is not something you grasp at desperately, fearful that if you loosen your grip, it will slip away. True love—whether found in another or within yourself—is something that stays effortlessly, something that does not require you to beg for its presence. I will no longer mistake longing for love. I will not accept half-hearted affection in the name of companionship. I will not settle for love that requires me to shrink, to mold myself into something smaller just to fit inside its arms. The love I choose for myself will be expansive, boundless. It will be steady, but it will also allow me to grow, to change, to continue becoming. Love should never ask you to stay the same; it should celebrate the evolution of who you are. And I will love again—not because I need to, but because I want to. Because love is not about filling a void but about overflowing from a place that is already full.

Stepping into the Future

The past does not define me. The pain does not suit me. The love I lost is not the end of my story. I step forward—not as someone who is missing a part of herself, but as someone who has found herself in space, she once thought was empty. But moving forward is not just about embracing what lies ahead, it is about acknowledging what I am leaving behind. I have made mistakes. I have hurt and been hurt. I have clung to love when I should have let go, grasped at fading light instead of embracing the darkness that would have allowed me to truly see myself. I have let fear dictate my choices, let uncertainty keep me bound to something that was no longer mine to hold. And I take responsibility for that now. I do not rewrite the past to make myself innocent, nor do I drown in the guilt of my own missteps. Instead, I choose to learn from them. I choose to accept that growth is messy, that healing is imperfect, that becoming better requires confronting the parts of yourself you once tried to ignore. I will not allow my mistakes to chain me to the past, but I will not erase them either. They are a part of my story, just as much as love and loss are. They have shaped me, taught me, pushed me toward the person I am still becoming. And so, as I step forward, I do so with awareness—with the knowledge that I am not perfect, but I am evolving. That I am not defined by where I have been, but by the choices I make now, in this moment, in this life that is still mine to live. I forgive myself for the things I did not know then. And I promise myself that moving forward, I will choose differently—not out of fear, not out of regret, but out of the love I have finally learned to give myself. Because stepping into the future is not about pretending the past did not happen. It is about proving that I am no longer the person who needed to stay there.

I am whole.

I am free.

I am ready.

13 The road beyond yesterday

There comes a time when the past no longer tugs at your sleeve, when the echoes of what began to fade into a distant hum rather than a relentless call. It doesn't happen all at once. It happens in fragments— On the way you wake up one morning and realize the ache in your chest is softer, no longer sharp and unforgiving. In the way a song that once shattered you now simply lingers for a moment before drifting away. In the way the name that once unraveled you no longer carries the weight of longing. It happens in the way you start moving through the world again—not as a ghost tied to what it was, but as someone reclaiming what is still theirs to live. It happens in the quietest ways, in the most unexpected places. And this was that time for me. The past had been my anchor for so long, holding me in place, keeping me tethered to something that no longer existed. But today, I felt lighter. Today, I let the past loosen its grip without fighting to hold onto it. Today, I turned toward something new.

A Life of My Own Making

I no longer measured my life by the love I once lost, nor did I seek meaning in the remnants of what had been. Instead, I began to build something new—not as a replacement, but as an expansion of who I was becoming. I filled my days with the things I once put aside. The books I had never finished. The cities I had never explored. The dreams I had once convinced myself were unreachable. I reclaimed what had been waiting for me all along—myself. There was a time when I thought love was the answer to everything, that its presence validated my existence. But now, I see that love, while beautiful, is not the foundation upon which I stand. I am the foundation. And I am enough. But building something new does not come without its challenges. There were days when doubt still crept in, when the past whispered that I was unworthy of a future untouched by regret. There were nights when I questioned whether I was truly capable of starting over, or if I was merely pretending to move forward while still glancing over my shoulder. Yet, each morning, I woke up and chose to begin again. To take one more step. Believing that the life I was creating was not just an illusion, but something real, something mine. The weight of the past did not disappear overnight. Some days, it still lingered in the background, like a quiet hum beneath the surface. But I no longer let it dictate my choices. I no longer let it hold me hostage. I had given myself permission to move on—not just physically, but emotionally, mentally, and spiritually.

Welcoming the Unknown

The future used to frighten me. It felt like a vast, open field, stretching far beyond my vision, and I feared stepping into it alone. But now, the unknown does not feel like an abyss—it feels like an invitation. An invitation to step beyond what I have known and embrace all that I have yet to discover. I no longer needed a hand to hold to steady myself. I had become my own anchor, my own compass, my own guide. I embraced the uncertainty not with hesitation, but with curiosity. Because the best parts of life were not found in what was left behind, but in what was still to come. There is a unique kind of peace in not knowing. In trusting that, even without a mapped-out plan, I will find my way. Uncertainty no longer feels like something to fear, but like a space waiting to be filled with new memories, new dreams, new possibilities. The unknown is no longer a void—it is a canvas, and I am the one holding the brush. I used to believe that security meant knowing exactly where I was going, that certainly was the only thing that could bring me peace. But I have learned that the most beautiful things in life are often the ones we do not anticipate, the ones we stumble upon when we finally release our grip on the past. There is freedom in surrendering control. In waking up without a rigid plan and instead allowing the day to unfold as it chooses. In letting the universe surprise, me, in saying yes to the unexpected, in trusting that I am exactly where I am meant to be. I welcome the unknown now, not as something to be conquered, but as something to be experienced. Because life is not meant to be perfectly mapped out, it is meant to be lived, step by step, moment by moment, without always knowing what comes next. And for the first time, I am okay with that.

The Journey Begins Again

I packed my bags, not as an escape, but as a step forward. I booked a one-way ticket to a place I had never been to, not to run from the past, but to run toward something new. As I stood at the airport, watching people move, lives intersecting and diverging, I realized something. This moment, this leap into the unknown—was not an ending. It was the beginning of a story I had yet to write. A story that belonged entirely to me. And I was ready to begin. With every step toward the gate, I felt the weight of my past lesson. I was no longer carrying the burden of what could have been; I was carrying the excitement of what was still possible. Maybe, for the first time in my life, I was writing a story that was not shaped by someone else's presence or absence. Perhaps, now, the only thing defining my next chapter was me. And maybe, just maybe, the best parts of my story were still ahead of me.

14 The city that doesn't know my name

A new city. A fresh beginning. A place where the past does not follow me, where my name is not tied to whispers of heartbreak or echoes of who I used to be.

I step onto the streets with no expectations. The cool air carried scents of unknown cuisine, and the distant hum of a bustling marketplace. The buildings rise tall and proud, their facades a mixture of old-world charm and modernity. There is no weight pressing against my chest, no ghosts lurking in the corners of familiar places. Here, I am a stranger. Here, I am free.

But freedom is not just about escaping the past. It is about stepping fully into the present, into the unknown, without fear of what is waiting on the other side. And this is what I am beginning to understand:

That the unknown does not have to be something I run from.

It can be something I run toward.

As I wander through the city, I am struck by its vibrancy. Street vendors call out their wares, children laugh as they chase each other through the parks, and the rhythm of life here feels like a heartbeat I am slowly syncing too. The architecture tells a story of resilience and progress, each building a testament to the city's evolution.

Belonging to Myself

I no longer wait for love to validate my existence. I no longer seek comfort in familiarity, in places that remind me of where I have been. Instead, I walk forward, embracing the unknown, letting the rhythm of this city become my own.

I found a small café on a quiet street, where no one knows my usual order, where no barista greets me with recognition. The aroma of freshly brewed coffee mingles with the scent of blooming flowers from a nearby florist. I take a seat by the window, sipping my coffee slowly, watching people pass-by-lives unfolding, stories continuing, each moment untouched by my past.

For the first time, I do not feel lost. I feel limitless. Because belonging is not about a place. It is not about being known or seen by others. It is about knowing and seeing yourself, about finding home within your own skin. And this is the truth I now know:

That I do not need to belong to someone else to feel like I belong at all.

As I explore more of the city, I stumble upon a hidden garden tucked away behind a row of townhouses. It is a serene oasis, with a small pond and benches shaded by weeping willows. I sit by the water's edge, watching the gentle ripples and feeling a sense of peace washing over me. This, too, is a part of my journey-finding solace in unexpected places, allowing the world to surprise me.

Learning to Start Over

Starting over is not about replacing what was lost. It is about creating something new, something different, something that belongs solely to me.

I explore streets I have never walked before, stepping into spaces that do not carry the weight of memory. The city's nightscape is equally mesmerizing, with streetlights casting a warm glow on cobblestone paths and jazz melodies drifting from dimly lit bars. I build new routines, allowing the present to shape me rather than the past. I let laughter escape from my lips, not because I am trying to convince myself I am happy, but because, for the first time in a long time, I simply am.

Some nights, the past still whispers. It reminds me of what I left behind, of the love that once held me, of the dreams I thought would last forever. But I do not let those whispers become chains. Instead, I acknowledge them, nod at them like old acquaintances, and then continue walking forward.

Because I am not who I used to be. And I do not want to be. The beauty of starting over is that it does not mean forgetting. It means carrying what once was with you-not as an anchor, but as a lesson. It means allowing yourself to change, to evolve, to become something new without guilt, without hesitation.

It means choosing yourself every single day.

I discovered a local art gallery, where vibrant paintings and sculptures reflect the city's diverse culture. Each piece tells a story, capturing the essence of human experience. I spend hours wandering through the exhibits, feeling inspired by the creativity that surrounds me.

The Beauty of the Unknown

This city does not know my name, and for once, I do not feel the need to be recognized. I do not need the past to define me, nor do I need validation from those who once knew me.

I am building a new life-not to prove anything to anyone, not to fill an empty space, but simply because I deserve it.

The unknown no longer frightens me. It welcomes me. And as I walk through the streets of this city that do not yet know my name, I realize that I am not lost at all.

I am exactly where I am meant to be.

I take a deep breath, feeling the cool air fill my lungs, feeling the world around me expand with possibility.

And then, with quiet certainty, I take my first step forward. Because the next chapter of my life is not something I am waiting for. It is something I am writing for myself.

Moments of Connection

In this city, I find myself forging new connections, not out of necessity, but out of genuine interest and curiosity. I strike up conversations with strangers in bookstores, attend poetry readings, and participate in community events. Each interaction adds a layer to my understanding of this place and to my sense of belonging.

One evening, I joined a local book club that meets in a cozy library. The discussions are lively, filled with diverse perspectives and passionate debates. I share my thoughts and listen to others, find common ground and appreciate the beauty of shared experiences.

In the warmth of these new connections, I realize that belonging is not about fitting into a mold or conforming to expectations. It is about being authentic, embracing who I am, and allowing others to see the real me.

A Journey of Self-Discovery

As the days turn into weeks, I continue to explore this city and myself. I take up photography, capturing moments of beauty and spontaneity that reflect my inner journey. Each photo becomes a piece of my story, a testament to my growth and resilience.

I visit the city's library, immersing myself in books that expand my horizons and challenge my thinking. The written word becomes a companion, guiding me through uncharted territories and offering solace during moments of uncertainty.

I also begin journaling, documenting my thoughts, feelings, and experiences. The pages of my journal become a safe space where I can reflect on my progress and celebrate my victories, no matter how small.

And as I stand on a bridge overlooking the city, watching the lights flicker like stars against the darkened skyline, I know one thing for certain-

This is not just a place I have come to escape. This is the place where I begin again.

15 The letter I never sent

Some words are never meant to be spoken aloud. Some letters are never meant to be sent. But sometimes, they must still be written.

Unraveling the Past

I sit by the window, the dim glow of a bedside lamp casting a golden hue over the blank page before me. The city outside hums with life, a stark contrast to the stillness inside my apartment. The pen feels heavy in my hand, as if it holds the weight of everything I have never said. I take a deep breath, steadying myself, and then I begin.

Lucian,

I don't know why I'm writing this. Perhaps it's because there are things I never got the chance to say. Possibly because, in some ways, I am still learning how to let go. Or it might be that I need to see these words outside of myself, to know that they exist somewhere other than my own mind.

There was a time when I believed love was unbreakable. That if we wanted something badly enough, if we held onto it tightly enough, it would never slip through our fingers. But love is not about possession. Love is not about clinging. It entails presence. And somewhere along the way, I lost sight of that.

I wanted you to know that I did love you. In all the ways I knew how. Even when I failed, even when I let fear dictate my choices, even when I convinced myself that I was unworthy of something as strong as what we had. And I know that saying this now changes nothing, but maybe this letter is not about changing the past.

Maybe it is about making peace with it.

The Words Left Unsaid

I pause, staring at the ink staining the page, my own handwriting a mirror of my heart—uneven, hesitant, but honest. There was a time when I thought closure meant rewriting the past, reshaping it into something more bearable. But I have come to understand that closure involves accepting what happened.

I pressed the pen to the paper again.

There were nights after you left when I wondered if I had imagined all of it—the love, the laughter, the way you used to look at me like I was the only person in the world. I tried to convince myself that maybe it wasn't as real as I thought it was, that maybe it was easier to pretend it hadn't meant as much as it did. But that was just another lie I told myself.

It was real. Every moment. Every whisper. Every time our hands reached for each other in the dark.

I carry those moments with me, not as regrets, but as lessons. You were my lesson in love, in loss, in learning that sometimes, the people we love are not meant to stay, no matter how much we want them to.

And maybe that is okay.

I think about the ways I tried to rewrite our ending in my mind. The times I convinced myself that if I had done something different, if I had fought harder, maybe things would not have ended the way they did. But I know now that love is not about winning or losing. It is not about who stayed and who walked away.

It is about the way we changed each other, for better or worse. And Lucian, you changed me.

Letting Go

The finality of that thought settles over me, not as something heavy, but as something freeing. I exhaled, feeling the weight I have carried for so long begin to lift.

I folded the letter carefully, as if it were something fragile, something sacred. I do not seal it. I do not address it. Because this letter was never meant to find its way to Lucian's hands.

It was meant to find its way back to me.

I stare at the folded pages, letting my fingers linger over them for a moment before placing them inside the drawer beside my bed. Not hidden. Not thrown away. Just… left where they belong. A part of my past, but no longer something I need to carry forward.

Letting go means freeing yourself from the need to hold on.

And tonight, for the first time, I set myself free.

Releasing the Past

The night is quiet as I step onto my balcony, the city sprawled before me, lights flickering like distant stars. I close my eyes, inhaling the crisp air, feeling something shifts inside me.

This is what it feels like to finally exhale.

I do not need to send this letter to be heard. I do not need to chase closure, because I have found it within myself.

The past does not define me. The love I lost is not the only love I will ever know.

I turn away from the city, stepping back inside. The letter remains in the drawer, untouched, unsent.

And I walk forward, unburdened, into whatever comes next.

Embracing the Future

The days blended into weeks, as I returned to the things I once loved but had abandoned. I pick up old hobbies, reconnect with friends, and allow myself to dream again. Life, with all its uncertainties and possibilities, feels new. I realize that the chapter with Lucian was just one part of my story, not its entirety.

Each sunrise brings with it a sense of renewal, a reminder that every ending is a new beginning. I let myself be vulnerable, to feel deeply, to embrace the beauty and pain of living fully. The scars from my past are not wounds to be hidden but marks of resilience and growth.

And as I stand on the precipice of this new chapter in my life, I do so with an open heart. Ready to face whatever comes next, knowing that I am stronger, wiser, and more compassionate because of my journey. The love I lost was never truly lost—it transformed me, guiding me toward a deeper understanding of myself and what it means to truly let go.

The path ahead is unwritten, but I am no longer afraid of the blank page. Instead, I am excited by the possibilities, by the stories yet to be told. And with each step forward, I carry the lessons of my past with me, not as burdens, but as testaments to my strength and capacity for love.

16 The loneliness that no longer scares me

Loneliness is not the absence of people. It is the presence of longing, the quiet ache of missing something you cannot name. It is the echo of laughter that is no longer there, the void left by conversations that have faded into memory. It is the haunting shadow that lingers, even in a crowded room, reminding you of the void within.

For a long time, I feared being alone. I equated solitude with emptiness, with the echoes of a past that refused to let me go. I filled the spaces around me with distractions, mistaking noise for comfort, mistaking company for love. The television blared incessantly, my phone buzzed with notifications, and my calendar was filled with social engagements I barely enjoyed. I surrounded myself with the cacophony of life, believing it would drown out the whispers of my heart. I feared that in the quiet, I would have to confront the parts of myself I kept hidden, even from myself.

But loneliness does not frighten me anymore. It has transformed from a menacing shadow lurking in the corners of my mind to a gentle presence that walks beside me, a constant reminder of my own resilience and capacity for growth. It is no longer an enemy to be feared but a companion to be embraced, guiding me towards a deeper understanding of myself.

Relearning Silence

At first, the silence was unbearable. It stretched between my thoughts like a vast, empty road, winding endlessly into the unknown. I filled it with meaningless conversations, with background noise, with anything that kept me from hearing the things I wasn't ready to face. I sought refuge in the mundane, fearing that the silence would force me to confront the ghosts of my past. The quiet was a mirror, reflecting the fears and insecurities I tried so hard to bury.

But one day, I let the silence stay. I did not turn on the television or call someone to fill the quiet. I let the stillness settle over me, and instead of fear, I found peace. In the absence of noise, I began to hear the gentle hum of my own existence. The quiet was no longer a void but a canvas upon which I could paint my thoughts and dreams.

There is something sacred in solitude, something I never allowed myself to embrace before. I sit by my window, watching the rain slip down the glass, and I feel no urgency to be anywhere else. Each drop tells a story, a journey from the heavens to the earth, and I am content to listen. The rhythm of the rain becomes a soothing melody, a reminder of the cyclical nature of life. I walk through the city alone, taking in the sights and sounds, and I do not feel like I am missing anything. The world moves around me, and for once, I do not feel left behind.

I am exactly where I need to be. In this silence, I have found a space where I can breathe, where my thoughts can roam freely without fear or judgment. The quiet has become a sanctuary, a place where I can be wholly and unapologetically myself.

The Difference Between Being Alone and Feeling Lonely

Loneliness signifies longing for something that is not there, a phantom ache that gnaws at the edges of your heart. It is a void that cannot be filled by mere presence, a yearning for connection that remains unfulfilled. It is the sense of being adrift, unanchored and untethered, searching for something or someone to ground you.

But being alone means simply existing in your own presence. It is the quiet contentment of knowing that you are enough, that your company is sufficient. I have come to understand that solitude is not a punishment; it is a gift. It is the space where I meet myself without distraction, where I learn who I am when no one else is watching. It is a sacred pause, a moment to breathe and reflect, unencumbered by the expectations and judgments of others.

I take myself out to dinner, sitting by a window where I can watch life pass by. The flickering candlelight casts a warm glow on my face, and I feel a sense of serenity. I order something new, something I have never tried before, and I savor it, not as an afterthought, but as a moment that belongs entirely to me. The flavors dance on my tongue, a symphony of tastes that I enjoy at my own pace.

There is a strange kind of freedom in learning to enjoy my own company, learning that I am enough. Each meal, each walk, each quiet moment is a testament to my self-discovery. It is in these small, seemingly insignificant moments that I find profound joy and contentment.

I used to believe that happiness was something given, something found in the presence of another. But I am learning now that happiness is something you create. It is in the way I wake up in the morning and make myself coffee, just for me. The aroma fills the room, a promise of a new day. It is in the long walks I take with no destination; on the way I allow myself to sit in silence without searching for something to fill it. It is in the books I read, the music I listen to, and the dreams I dare to dream.

This is what it means to belong to yourself. It is the realization that you are your own best companion, that your worth is not determined by others. It is a profound understanding of who you are, with all your flaws and imperfections, and a celebration of the journey you have undertaken to get here.

Finding Wholeness Without Another

For so long, I waited for someone to make me feel whole, to complete the puzzle of my existence. I believed that without another, I was only half a person, lost and incomplete. I searched for validation in the eyes of others, hoping they would see in me what I struggled to see in myself.

But now, I see that I was never incomplete. I never miss a piece. I was simply waiting to see myself clearly, to understand that I have always been enough on my own. The search for wholeness was a journey inward, a path that led me back to myself. It was a revelation, a moment of clarity that changed everything.

I fill my days with things that bring me joy—not because they distract me, but because they are mine. I take up painting, letting colors bleed across the canvas without rules, without expectation. Each brushstroke is an expression of my soul, a dance of hues and shades. I read poetry late into the night, whispering words that feel like they were written just for me. The verses become my lullabies, a soothing balm for my spirit. I dance in my apartment, barefoot and unafraid, moving only for myself. The music flows through me, a symphony of self-acceptance.

And for the first time, I am not waiting for someone to witness me. I do not need validation from others to feel complete. I have learned to be my own witness, to celebrate my own victories and mourn my own losses.

I am enough, even when no one is watching. My worth is inherent, a truth that needs no external affirmation. I am whole, complete in my own existence, a tapestry of experiences and emotions that I alone have woven.

The Loneliness That No Longer Scares Me

There are still nights when the past knocks at my door, when memories creep in like unwelcome visitors. They whisper of regret, missed opportunities, and lost connections. But I do not let them take up space. I acknowledge them, then let them drift away, like leaves carried by the wind. They are a part of my story, but they do not define me.

Quiet no longer frightens me. It is a canvas on which I paint my dreams and aspirations. The stillness of my own presence holds no terror. It is a sanctuary where I find solace and strength. The quiet is no longer a void to be filled, but a space to be cherished.

Because I have learned that being alone does not mean being unloved. Love is not confined to the presence of others; it is a state of being that begins within. It is the gentle kindness I show myself, the patience I extend to my own journey, the compassion I offer for my own struggles.

And being with myself is not something I endure is something I cherish. It is a celebration of my existence, a testament to my resilience and growth. I am my own companion, my own source of comfort and joy. The loneliness that once haunted me has transformed into a profound sense of belonging, a connection to the deepest parts of myself.

In this journey of self-discovery, I have found a truth that resonates within me: I am enough. I always have been, and I always will be. The loneliness that once scared me has become a friend, guiding me towards a deeper understanding of who I am and who I am meant to be.

17 The love that feels like freedom

Love can sometimes feel like gravity: heavy, inescapable, and pulling one toward something uncertain. It involves longing and loss, holding and breaking, balancing the desire for someone to stay with the fear of their departure. This form of love comes with uncertainty, demands parts of oneself that may be challenging to offer, and sometimes feels more like a tether than a gift. However, it is argued that love should not feel like gravity, but rather like the skylight: expansive and open. It should allow movement, free breathing, and reaching for greater things without fear.

Redefining Love

The belief that loves means finding another half, filling empty spaces, or having a hand to hold in darkness is questioned. Instead, love is described as two whole people standing side by side, choosing each other out of joy rather than necessity. Embracing solitude and self-acceptance is emphasized, asserting that true love does not require changing oneself, proving worth, or shrinking. It allows individuals to exist fully and build a shared space where both can thrive without taking and holding too tightly. True love is unconditional, expansive, and supports both individuals' growth while maintaining their autonomy.

Love is viewed as two complete individuals choosing each other, not out of dependency, but from a place of joy. The importance of embracing solitude and understanding its value is highlighted, recognizing that real love allows one to be authentically themselves. Love should not demand sacrifices or the silencing of dreams and voices but should create a space where both individuals coexist fully and freely. Real love is not about completing oneself through another but about enhancing each other's lives without possession or control. It emphasizes freedom and choice, where love allows personal growth and autonomy while being a shared journey.

A Love Without Fear

If love were to come again, ideally, it would feel like laughter, sunlight, and unhurried moments. It would be unforced, moving in rhythm together, chosen freely rather than needed. Love would not be seen as the missing piece or final chapter, but as a part of the journey. The preference for a love that is quietly confident and steady through difficulties is expressed, suggesting that love should encourage growth, not hinder it. If love does not come, finding joy and contentment within oneself remains paramount. Love is seen as something to be welcomed, cherished, and released if it asks for less than one's true self. It is suggested that real love never demands changing one's essence.

The importance of choosing love based on trust and encouragement for growth is emphasized. Love should be steady and unwavering, neither questioning worth nor hindering personal aspirations. Whether or not love arrives, the focus is on living a full life independently. Love is viewed not as a necessity, but as an addition to happiness, complementing rather than defining oneself. The narrative shifts toward valuing self-love and individual completeness without relying on external validation.

Letting Love Find Me

The approach to love has changed from actively searching to embracing self-worth and choosing oneself. Self-measurement of love includes greeting the day positively, contentment in solitude, laughter, nurturing friendships, and giving warmth freely. This perspective views love as not something to chase, but as something that naturally exists between two people who choose each other joyfully. Love is no longer seen as a destination, but as a possible encounter along the journey, complementing rather than defining oneself. If love adds to happiness, it will walk alongside rather than carry one. The emphasis is on building a fulfilling life independently and recognizing self-love as the most powerful form of love.

In conclusion, love is perceived as a choice made freely by two whole individuals. It should enhance both lives without demanding sacrifices or control. Whether love finds one or not, self-sufficiency and contentment are paramount. The journey of self-love and individual completeness is recognized as the foundation for any future love that might come.

18 I write for myself

I have spent so much of my life living in the pages of someone else's story. I have played roles I did not choose, followed narratives I did not write, shaped myself to fit expectations that were never truly mine. I have been the lover, the friend, the woman who stayed and left, the one who loved too much, and the one who feared love altogether. I have lived in spaces between people, waiting for them to tell me who I was, waiting for them to define my worth. But now, I am ready to write my own chapter. And for the first time, I do not need anyone else to hold the pen.

Choosing My Own Path

For so long, I waited. I waited for love, for clarity, for the moment when everything would suddenly make sense. I waited for someone to tell me I was enough, for life to prove to me that I was worthy. I let the waiting define me, believing that the next step, the next relationship, the next revelation, the next destination—would be the thing that finally completed me. But life is not about waiting. It is about choosing. So, I choose myself. I choose to wake up each morning and greet the day as it is, not as I wish it to be. I choose to take risks, to embrace change, to step into the unknown without fear. I choose to stop looking for signs and start listening to my own voice. I choose to trust myself—not because I have all the answers, but because I am no longer afraid of making mistakes. At last, I am not searching for something outside of myself. I am writing my own story, and I am enough.

The Beauty of an Unwritten Future

There was a time when uncertainty terrified me. When I needed to know how the story ended before I could allow myself to begin. I wanted guarantees, promises, a path laid out before me, free of risk and regret. But life does not come with certainty. And I am learning that this is a gift. The unwritten future is not something to fear, it is something to create. It is a canvas stretched wide before me, waiting for color, for movement, for bold strokes of passion and purpose. It is the openness of possibility, the freedom to reinvent, to evolve, to change my mind as many times as I need to. I no longer crave a love that comes with guarantees. I do not need a plan set in stone. I do not need the comfort of knowing exactly where I am going. I only need to know that I am the one deciding where to go next.

A Story Worth Telling

This chapter focuses on me. It is about the woman who finally realized she was enough all along. The woman who no longer waits for permission to take up space. The woman who chooses herself, every single day, in ways both small and profound. It is about the nights she spent alone, not as something to be endured, but as something to be cherished. It is about the laughter she found in solitude, the joy she uncovered in the simplest of moments. It is about the way she finally looked in the mirror and did not wish to be anyone else. This is not the end of my story. This is just the beginning. And for the first time, I am the one writing it.

19 Breaking free from lies

The lies that keep us in limbo

The city lights blur as I speed down the highway, the engine roaring a symphony of defiance against the silence that threatens to engulf me. The road ahead stretches into the darkness, a metaphor for the uncertain path I've chosen, a path leading away from the lies that have held me captive for far too long.

A lifetime was spent building walls, constructing fortresses around my heart, shielding myself from the vulnerability love demands. I've worn masks of indifference, pretending that I don't need connection, that I don't crave intimacy, that I am complete on my own.

But the truth is, I am not.

The lie that I am self-sufficient, that I don't need anyone, has been my constant companion, a shield against the pain of rejection, the fear of abandonment. But it has also been a barrier, preventing me from experiencing the fullness of love, the joy of true connection.

Tonight, I am breaking free from that lie.

Flashback

I remember a time when I believed that love was a weakness, a vulnerability to being avoided at all costs. I witnessed my parents' tumultuous relationship, their bitter arguments, their tearful reconciliations. I had vowed never to allow myself to be that vulnerable, that dependent on another person.

I built walls around my heart, convinced that I could protect myself from pain by keeping others at bay. But in doing so, I also closed myself off from the possibility of love, the joy of connection, the fulfillment of intimacy.

It wasn't until I met Alina that I began to question my beliefs about love. She challenged my cynicism, broke through my defenses, and showed me the beauty of vulnerability, the power of connection.

But even as I fell in love with her, I clung to my old patterns, my fear of intimacy, my need for control. And in the end, my fear drove her away.

Lucian's Perspective

The memory of my past mistakes, my misguided beliefs about love, fuels my determination to change, to embrace vulnerability, to open my heart to the possibility of true connection.

I know that the road ahead will not be easy. There will be moments of doubt, of fear, of temptation to retreat back into the safety of my old patterns. But I will not give in.

Committing to breaking free from the lies that held me captive, I will live authentically, embracing my true self, loving and being loved without reservation.

Internal Monologue

The city lights reflect in the rearview mirror, a kaleidoscope of colors that mirror the kaleidoscope of emotions swirling within me. I am filled with a mix of excitement, trepidation, and a deep sense of hope.

I am excited about the possibilities that lie ahead, the chance to create a new life, a new love, a new future. But I am also afraid, afraid of making the same mistakes, of falling back into old patterns, of failing to live up to my own expectations.

But through it all, I feel a sense of hope, a belief that I am capable of change, that I am worthy of love, that I am destined for a life filled with joy, meaning, and fulfillment.

Lucian's Perspective

I pull over to the side of the road, the silence of the night enveloping me like a comforting embrace. I step out of the car, the cool air a welcome contrast to the heat of the engine.

I look up at the stars, their twinkling light, a reminder of the vastness of the universe, the endless possibilities that exist beyond my own limited perspective.

I close my eyes and take a deep breath, feeling the earth beneath my feet, the wind against my skin, the silence filling my senses.

In this moment, I am present, fully present, connected to the world around me, to the universe within me.

And in this moment, I know that I am not alone.

I continue my drive, the road ahead stretching out before me like a ribbon of hope. I don't know where I'm going, but I know that I am on the right path. I am following my heart, my intuition, my inner compass.

I am trusting that the universe will guide me, that it will lead me to where I need to be, to the people I am meant to meet, to the experiences that will shape me, mold me, and transform me.

I am open to the possibilities, to adventures, to the unknown.

For I know that the greatest joys in life often lie hidden in the most unexpected places.

Lucian's Perspective

The lie that I am self-sufficient, that I don't need anyone, is fading, dissolving into the darkness like a distant star.

I am embracing my vulnerability, my need for connection, my desire to love and be loved.

I am shedding the masks, the pretenses, the defenses that have kept me from experiencing the fullness of life.

I am becoming the man I was always meant to be, the man who is authentic, compassionate, and courageous.

The man who is not afraid to love, to trust, to let go. The man who is writing his own chapter, a chapter filled with truth, beauty, and the boundless possibilities of a life lived to the fullest.

20 The road ahead

Lucian's Perspective

The sun dips below the horizon, painting the sky with streaks of fiery orange, crimson, and gold. I stand on the rooftop of my office building, the city spread out before me like a shimmering tapestry of dreams.

The air is alive with the sounds of the city – the rumble of traffic, the distant sirens, the laughter and chatter of people enjoying the warm summer evening. But above all, I hear the steady beat of my own heart, a rhythm of resilience, determination, and unwavering hope.

The road behind me is long and winding, paved with both triumphs and failures, joys and sorrows. But I don't look back. My gaze is fixed on the horizon, on the endless possibilities that lie ahead.

My choices, actions, and unwavering commitment to creating a meaningful and fulfilling life define me. I am no longer defined by my losses, by my heartbreaks, by the ghosts of yesterday.

Flashback

I remember a time when I believed that success was the key to happiness. I chased it relentlessly, sacrificing everything else in my life – my relationships, my health, my own well-being.

I climbed the corporate ladder, amassed a fortune, and achieved a level of success that most people only dream of. But it wasn't enough.

The emptiness within me remained, a gaping void that couldn't be filled by money, power, or prestige.

It wasn't until I lost everything – my love, my career, my sense of self – that I finally realized the truth.

Success without fulfillment is meaningless.

Lucian's Perspective

The memory of that realization still stings a reminder of the price I paid for my misguided ambition.

But through experience, I now understand to define success on my own terms, to pursue goals that align with my values and passions, to create a life that is both challenging and rewarding.

I've come to realize that true happiness comes from within, from self-acceptance, from meaningful connections, from living a life that is true to myself.

And so, I stand here today, on the cusp of a new chapter, my heart filled with gratitude, hope, and a sense of boundless possibility.

A New Beginning

The city lights twinkle below, a reflection of the dreams and aspirations that fill my heart. I am surrounded by the evidence of my success – the towering skyscrapers, the bustling streets, the vibrant energy that permeates the air.

But my focus is not on the past, nor is it solely on the present. I am looking ahead, to the future, to the endless possibilities that await me.

I envision a world where technology is used to empower and connect people, to solve global challenges, and to create a more just and sustainable future. I see myself at the forefront of this movement, leading the charge, inspiring others, and making a lasting impact on the world.

I am driven by a deep sense of purpose, a desire to leave a legacy that extends beyond myself, a legacy that will inspire future generations to dream big, to take risks, and to never give up on their passions.

The journey, I also know, is just as important as the destination. I am committed to living a life that is both fulfilling and meaningful, a life that reflects my values, my passions, and my vision for the future.

I am embracing the uncertainty, the unknown, the adventure of it all.

For I know that the best is yet to come.

Epilogue

The symphony of self

The city lights shimmer like a symphony of stars, a breathtaking nocturne composed by the rhythm of life itself. I stand on the precipice of a new dawn, the past a distant melody fading into the embrace of time.

The journey has been a symphony of its own, a concerto of highs and lows, of crescendos and diminuendos, of moments that have shaped me, molded me, and transformed me into the man I am today.

I stand as Lucian, the driven, the resilient, the unyielding. I am the composer of my own symphony, the conductor of my own destiny.

The notes of my past, the chords of my experiences, the melodies of my relationships – they have all played a part in creating the symphony of my life.

But the music is not over yet. There are still movements to be written, themes to be explored, harmonies to be discovered.

I am eager to see what the next movement holds, what new melodies will emerge, what harmonies will resonate within my soul.

The Maestro of My Fate

Now, I am the maestro of my own fate, the conductor of my own destiny. I hold the baton, and I guide the orchestra of my life, shaping the music, creating the symphony that reflects my deepest desires, my passions, and my vision for the future.

The tempo may change, the rhythm may shift, the melody may evolve. But the music will always be mine, a unique and beautiful expression of my soul.

I am not afraid of the dissonances, the unexpected chords, the moments of discord. For I know that they are all part of the symphony, that they add depth and complexity to the music.

I embrace the challenges, the uncertainties, the unknown. For I know that they are all opportunities for growth, for transformation, for creating a symphony that is both beautiful and meaningful.

The Symphony of Self

The symphony of self is a lifelong composition, a work in progress that is constantly evolving, growing, and changing.

This symphony encompasses love, of loss, of joy, of sorrow, of all the emotions and experiences that make us human.

Life's symphony includes dreams, aspirations, and hopes, all the things that make life worth living.

It is a symphony of self-discovery, of transformation, of becoming the best version of ourselves.

The symphony of connection, of community, of the shared human experience that binds us together.

It is a symphony of life, a celebration of the journey, a testament to the resilience of the human spirit.

Music Never Ends

The music never ends. It flows through us, around us, connecting us to something greater than ourselves.

It is the rhythm of the universe, the heartbeat of creation, the song of existence.

And as I stand here, on the cusp of a new beginning, I am filled with a sense of gratitude, awe, and wonder.

I am grateful for the music of my life, for the symphony of self that is still being written.

I am in awe of the beauty and complexity of the universe, of the infinite possibilities that lie ahead.

And I am filled with wonder at the mystery and magic of life, of the journey that is still unfolding.

Lucian's Legacy

The city lights twinkle like a million fallen stars, a reminder of the countless lives that are intertwined with my own. I am but one instrument in the grand orchestra of humanity, one voice in the chorus of existence.

But my music matters. My story matters. My life matters.

I am determined to make my contribution to the symphony, to leave a legacy that will inspire and uplift others, to create a world that is more just, more compassionate, and more harmonious.

Today, I am Lucian, the driven, the resilient, the unyielding.

And this is my symphony.

Afterword

And now, we have reached the end. But not the kind that leaves you empty—rather, the kind that feels like a beginning.

If this book found you in a moment of uncertainty, of heartbreak, of searching for yourself in the spaces love once occupied, I hope it reminded you of something essential: you were never lost to begin with. You were always here, waiting for the moment you would finally choose yourself.

This story was never just mine—it was always yours, too. Because we have all stood at the crossroads of love and self-worth, wondering if choosing ourselves means losing something greater. But the truth is, choosing yourself is the greatest love story you will ever write.

So, as you close these pages, I hope you walk away knowing that you are enough—not when someone else sees it, not when love finally arrives, but now, as you are, in this very moment.

Thank you for allowing me to share this journey with you. And if you ever forget your own worth, may these words find you again, whispering what you already know deep inside:

You are worthy. You are whole. You are home.

— Kessa Alcenat

ABOUT THE AUTHOR

Kessa Alcenat is a writer with a passion for exploring the intricate tapestry of human emotions and experiences. He believes that stories have the power to heal, inspire, and connect us, offering glimpses into the depths of the human heart and the resilience of the human spirit. His writing delves into the complexities of love, loss, and the transformative journey of self-discovery, inviting readers to reflect on their own lives and the choices that shape their destinies.

He is the author of the debut novel, "The Night, I Chose Myself," a captivating story of heartbreak, betrayal, and redemption, set against the backdrop of a bustling city and the quiet solitude of the human soul. The novel follows the journey of Lucian, a driven and ambitious man who must confront his deepest fears and insecurities as he navigates the treacherous terrain of love, loss, and the courage to choose himself.

When he's not crafting compelling narratives, Kessa finds solace and inspiration in the embrace of nature. He enjoys hiking through lush forests, kayaking on serene lakes, and simply sitting under a starry sky, contemplating the mysteries of the universe. He also finds creative expression through music, composing melodies that capture the emotions and experiences that words sometimes fail to convey.

Kessa believes that life is a journey of self-discovery, a continuous exploration of the world within and the world around us. He is passionate about sharing his stories and insights with readers, hoping to inspire them to embrace their own journeys, to overcome their challenges, and to create lives filled with purpose, passion, and authenticity.